LISA KESSLER

SONG OF
the soul

Book #7 of the Muse Chronicles

LISA KESSLER

Song of the Soul – Copyright © 2018 by Lisa Kessler
Print Edition

All rights reserved, including the right to reproduce, distribute, or transmit in any form or by any means. For information regarding subsidiary rights, please contact the Author.

This book is a work of fiction. Names, characters, places, and incidents are the product of the author's imagination or are used fictitiously. Any resemblance to actual events, locales, or persons, living or dead, is coincidental.

Visit Lisa's website: Lisa-Kessler.com
Sign up for Lisa's newsletter: goo.gl/56lDla

Edited by Double Vision Editorial, Danielle Poiesz
Cover design by Fiona Jayde Media
Interior Design by – BB eBooks
Vase Icon made by Freepik from www.flaticon.com is licensed under CC BY 3.0

Manufactured in the United States of America First Edition November 2018

Other Novels by Lisa Kessler

The Muse Chronicles
LURE OF OBSESSION
LEGEND OF LOVE
BREATH OF PASSION
LIGHT OF THE SPIRIT
DEVOTED TO DESTINY
DANCE OF THE HEART
SONG OF THE SOUL

The Night Series
NIGHT WALKER
NIGHT THIEF
NIGHT DEMON
NIGHT ANGEL
NIGHT CHILD

The Moon Series
MOONLIGHT
HUNTER'S MOON
BLOOD MOON
HARVEST MOON
ICE MOON
BLUE MOON
WOLF MOON
NEW MOON

The Sedona Pack
SEDONA SIN
SEDONA SEDUCTION

The Sentinels of Savannah
MAGNOLIA MYSTIC
PIRATE'S PASSION

Summerland Stories
ACROSS THE VEIL
FORBIDDEN HEARTS

Stand Alone Works
BEG ME TO SLAY
FORGOTTEN TREASURES

Dedication

This one is for Ray Bradbury...
This series never would have happened without you.

CHAPTER 1

Trinity Porter twisted the tuning peg on her guitar as she scanned the crowd of elite guests milling about the Crystal City Observatory. She strummed her thumb across the strings and made a couple more adjustments until her ear approved of the tone of the open chord.

Her sisters should have been there by now. They weren't sisters by blood, but all of them had been led to Crystal City by prophetic dreams for the same purpose: restoring and reopening *Les Neuf Soeurs*, the Theater of the Muses. Eventually, they had come to learn that they each embodied one of the nine daughters of Zeus. They were each vessels inspired by the muse inside her soul. And Trinity was the human vessel for Euterpe, the Muse of Music. Other than her and her sisters, there were only two people at this black-tie event that knew the Greek muses walked among them. And she had no intention of speaking to either of them.

She had only accepted the invitation to entertain at tonight's gala because the new telescope they were unveiling, a gift from Mikolas Leandros to the city, was being named after her friend, Nia Miller. Nia, the Muse of Astronomy, was the light of their sisterhood, but her life was cut short by fanatics in black robes and gold masks. Her murder still haunted Trinity. And no amount of money, or memorials in her name, would bring Nia back.

"Hey, Trin." Erica approached wearing a flashy red dress that accentuated every curve of her full-figured body.

"Hi, Erica. I was starting to worry."

Erica was also Erato, the Muse of Lyrics and Erotic Poetry. She and Trinity used to be roommates before Erica found her Guardian, got married, and had an adorable baby girl. Trinity was happy for her, of course, but it was lonely being the only Muse without a Guardian.

"He hasn't come by to talk to you?" Erica asked, keeping her voice low as she skimmed the crowd for the rich Greek who had donated the telescope. "He swooped in, stopped Kronos, and now he's immortalizing Nia with a telescope." She turned to Trinity again. "Maybe he's not the bad guy we think he is."

"Well I'm not going to talk to him and find out. No more men for me, thanks." Trinity tipped her head toward the way-too-sexy-for-his-own-good billionaire staring at her from the other side of the champagne fountain. "He's over there. Do me a favor and keep him busy."

Erica followed her gaze and sighed. "Damn. He looks even better in a tux."

"Yeah." Trinity focused on her instrument, readjusting the microphone pointed at the hole in the center of her guitar. "I still don't want to speak to him."

"I know. I'm on it." She started to go but then turned back. "You know we'd all be dead right now if Mikolas hadn't sent Kronos back to Tartarus."

"Maybe." Trinity narrowed her eyes at Erica. "But it won't bring back Nia or Polly."

"I know, but still…" She glanced around the room and back to Trinity. "Ted Belkin is supposed to be here someplace, too."

Ted Belkin. Just hearing his name added weight to the guilt on Trinity's shoulders. Ted's father had been the leader of the Order of the Titans, the guys in the robes and masks that murdered Nia. Ted had also been her boyfriend in college. Huge mistake.

"Lia and Cooper are covering him."

Erica cocked a brow. "You have this all planned out."

Trinity almost smiled as she shrugged. "I'm here to make music. I'm not dealing with any other bullshit. Tonight is for Nia."

Erica nodded. "Break a leg, Trin."

Trinity strummed her guitar and gave the sound guy a thumbs-up. The mic went live, and she leaned into it. "Good evening. I'm Trinity Porter. Thanks to the Friends of the Crystal City Observatory for inviting me to be here tonight."

Her playlist for the night featured a couple of covers, a few tunes off her most recent album, and a song she and Erica had written together to celebrate Nia's life, "Starlight."

Trinity started playing and lost herself in the music, allowing the muse inside her soul to take over. The crowd faded away until only the song remained. Her voice joined the melody, weaving emotions into a tapestry of song.

Heaven.

THE EMOTION THAT filled her songs tore at Mikolas like a fist clenching around his heart. The smooth notes from her guitar blended with her smoky voice, and slid under his skin, kindling the pain and regret lurking deep in his soul.

A redhead in a slinky red dress approached. She picked up a champagne glass and tipped it into the fountain.

"Did she send you over here to distract me?" Mikolas sipped his drink without taking his gaze off Trinity.

She lifted her glass. "Yes."

He forced his attention away from the songstress in the center of the room and looked at her friend. "So she's smart *and* beautiful."

Erica nodded slowly. "Yeahhh." She cleared her throat. "I'm Erica, by the way."

"I know who you are." He'd spent the past year undercover, infiltrating the Order of the Titans. He'd taken charge and insisted that there would be no more muse killing. The muses were well aware he'd been leading the Order, so she had to know that he not only knew their names but where they lived and worked, too. There was no sense playing games about it.

He focused on Trinity again. All this time he'd believed he'd been marked to be the Guardian of the Muse of Astronomy as his grandfather had been before him. And for months, he'd thought he'd failed Nia. She had already been killed by the time he'd arrived in Crystal City, and he'd punished himself for so long, he wasn't sure how to end the self-loathing.

It wasn't until the day he'd sent Kronos back to his prison in Tartarus that he had realized he'd been wrong. The second he had discovered Trinity backstage at the theater after the dance recital, his crescent-shaped birthmark burned, a sign he'd found his muse. In his panic to save her from Kronos, he'd plunged a crystal shard into the back of the Father of the Gods, banishing him from this world.

But saving her hadn't changed her perception of him. He'd been the leader of the Order of the Titans, the fanatics that killed her friends, and part of him accepted her disdain.

Erica cleared her throat. "So how about blending into the crowd and leaving her alone tonight?"

"I have no intention of interrupting her." He sipped his champagne. "However, did you notice our uninvited guest?" He pointed to an older gentleman in a purple hooligan hat. "Now that we've cleaned up his mess, he's suddenly ready to support his daughters."

Erica sighed. "Zack Vrontios is Agnes Hanover's ride. She doesn't know his real identity. To her, he's just a sweet guy in her retirement community."

"And Agnes is…?" Mikolas took another sip of his champagne.

"She's Cooper's grandmother, and her generation's Muse of Hymns."

He frowned. "And Zack drives her around without mentioning he's really…Polyhymnia's father?"

Erica clicked her glass to his. "You know your muses."

"I do." He glanced over at her as he knocked back the rest of his drink. "What I don't know is why Zack keeps up this disguise. We know who he really is. The mighty Zeus hides in our world in the form of an elderly man like a coward." Mikolas shook his head. "He has no business being here tonight. He could have stopped the Order of the Titans with a wave of his hand. Nia didn't have to die."

"I agree on that final point." Erica raised a brow, her hip jutting to the side. "Look, it sounds like you've got a lot of unresolved issues with Zack, but all *I* care about is that you respect Trin's wishes and keep your distance."

He clenched his jaw and nodded.

"Thanks." Erica made her way through the crowd

back to her friends, leaving Mikolas alone.

He glared at Zack until the old man finally turned. Their gazes locked for a moment before he made his way over to Mikolas.

The mighty Zeus. Using a cane.

Mikolas rolled his eyes as Zack stopped beside him. Zack tugged at the brim of his purple hat. "I think we need to talk."

Mikolas crossed his arms. "I have nothing to say to you."

"That's fine. I can talk for both of us." Zeus chuckled. "I wanted to thank you for protecting my daughters from my father's ambush."

Mikolas narrowed his eyes at the deity masquerading as a harmless retiree. "I didn't know if the shard would work. They all could have died. How many would he have tortured before you finally broke out of this mortal disguise and protected them? The Guardians' prophecy calls the muses your treasure, but you have a sick way of showing it, old man."

"Well…" Zack cocked a silver brow. "You found something to say after all."

Mikolas cursed under his breath, focusing on Trinity again. "Why are you still here?"

"Because Trinity is special to me." He touched Mikolas's shoulder, and all Mikolas's muscles contracted, the energy knotting under his skin and stealing his breath. Zack lowered his voice. "I bestowed a piece of my power in your heart while you were in your mother's womb. I expect you to use it. The danger hasn't passed; Trinity is vulnerable unless you're at her side."

Zack released him, and Mikolas sucked in a deep breath, frowning. "What the hell are you talking about? Kronos was banished to Tartarus, and the Order of the Titans was defeated. The fight is over."

Mikolas gestured toward the songstress in the center of the Observatory. "And even if it weren't, she hates me, and with good reason. She thinks I ordered the fire that nearly killed all of them. I couldn't tell her anything more at the time without losing the influence I had over the Order and your father's mistress, Philyra. The battles *you* chose to hide from."

"You think the danger has passed? Far from it." Something sparked in the old man's bright-blue eyes. Power. Raw and primal. For a moment, the visage of the old man melted away to reveal Zeus's true form, his lightning bolt clenched in a tight fist. Fear stirred in Mikolas's stomach, but when he blinked, Zack was there again.

"Tell me something, Mikolas," he whispered. "My mother's shard banished Kronos back to Tartarus, but he's already breached the prison in the Earth's core once. What's to stop him from doing it again? Maybe this time, he'll even bring some of his Titan brethren with him."

A chill shot through Mikolas, and his gaze snapped to Trinity. "Will you help me protect her?"

"You and the other Guardians have the gifts to

keep them safe. Work together while I deal with Kronos. He can't be killed, and now that he can escape from Tartarus, there's no place we can trap him, either. If he brings another Titan through to this world, you and the Guardians will need to handle it until I've settled things with my father."

"I have the Guardian's mark—" Mikolas looked over at Zack "—but I don't have a gift. My birthmark burned when Trinity was in danger, but nothing awakened inside me. The other Guardians have super strength, incredible speed, mind reading, or telekinesis. Nothing changed when I found my muse."

Zack smirked. "No human could have wielded the shard. It would have killed you instantly when you touched it."

What the hell was the old man talking about?

Suddenly, a memory awoke within him. "Rhea. Your mother. She took the shard from me after Kronos vanished. She said I shouldn't have been able to hold it, but before I could ask her anything, she was gone."

Zack squeezed his forearm. This time there was no electrical charge. His voice dropped to a whisper. "I already told you, a piece of my power bloomed in your heart before you were born. It took finding Trinity to awaken it. You're a demigod, Mikolas."

Mikolas blinked in disbelief, struggling to find words. "Like Achilles or... Are you saying I can throw lightning bolts like you can?"

"No lightning bolts, and you aren't impervious to

wounds either." Zack chuckled. "But you can harness divine power. You can channel it without harming your mortal body."

Mikolas rubbed his forehead, struggling to make sense of this new information. "I don't understand."

"You will." Zack leaned on his golden cane. "Be alert." He looked over at Trinity, a wistful curve to his lips. "She carries around almost as much guilt as you do, my boy." His eyes locked on Mikolas again. "Be good to her and keep her safe."

He turned and made his way through the crowd much more quickly than his aged physical form should've allowed. Mikolas replayed the conversation in his mind, trying to digest the meaning, but Trinity's voice cut through and calmed the storm.

"This is a new song for our friend, Nia. It's called 'Starlight.'" She glanced to the heavens and then strummed her guitar.

> *"We're made from stardust, so they say,*
> *"Though you shone brighter than the stars each day.*
> *"Now you're gone, but your shadow lingers.*
> *"The light snuffed out by unseen fingers.*
>
> *"We look to the stars, they twinkle and shine,*
> *"People make wishes and beg the divine.*
> *"But they don't know the magic of your smile,*
> *"Or the inspiration you poured out by the mile.*

"You were our starlight.
"Our magic and joy.
"Even the darkness can't hide you.
"You still sparkle and glow,
"So the world will know.
"Hope still lives…in the starlight."

The chorus swelled, her pain laid bare, and Mikolas couldn't find words to describe the spell she'd cast over the crowd. The final verse was quiet but full of hope, and when the last chord faded into the ether, silence clung to the room for a moment. Gradually, applause broke out, and Mikolas joined in as Zeus's warning crept back into his mind.

Tartarus wouldn't be able to hold Kronos.

If Zack was right, the Father of the Gods would return to Crystal City, and his righteous anger could destroy the entire world. No amount of inspiration would be able to save them.

TED BELKIN TUGGED at his bow tie as he finished off his Vodka Collins. He placed the glass on the catering tray a little harder than he'd intended to. No amount of alcohol could deaden the ache inside when he listened to Trinity sing. He could drown under the weight of his regrets. He'd made so many mistakes—colossal errors in judgment.

There was no way to atone for his actions. Sure, he had excuses. His sick desire to please his father, his eagerness to avenge his father's death, and that didn't even scratch the surface when it came to Pamela. She'd hidden herself among the humans and driven the Order of the Titans to murder. Her true identity, Philyra—Kronos's mistress—was realized much too late. She had played Ted like a fiddle.

The only good to come from the past two years had been his tenuous allegiance with Mikolas Leandros. The Greek businessman had become the closest thing Ted had to a friend since his father's death. And now even that one bright spot was being tarnished.

He'd earned this karma, he understood that, but dammit, that didn't make tonight any easier.

When Mikolas arrived in Crystal City, he'd been convinced his muse was dead and had struggled to compensate for his failure to save Nia, only to find his true muse: Trinity. It was fucking cruel, but did he deserve any better? Probably not.

Mikolas hadn't planned for it to happen. The gods did. They let Mikolas believe he'd failed his muse, but in the end, he hadn't been marked to be Nia's Guardian at all. The gods had chosen the Greek to be the protector of the Muse of Melody.

Ted watched Trinity strum her guitar, her voice reaching right into his chest, clutching his heart. God, he needed another drink.

She'd been his once. His first love. She had made him believe he could chase his dreams instead of following in his father's footsteps. She'd inspired him to be more. And he'd gone and repaid her by dumping her, skipping town, and betraying her and her muse sisters to his father and the Order of the Titans.

He shook his head as he headed for the bar. He'd tried to make amends, to help the muses fight Kronos, but it would never bring back Nia or Polly. And it would never change the fact that Zeus had marked Ted's only friend to be the protector of the only woman Ted had ever loved.

"Another please." He laid a crisp twenty-dollar bill on the bar.

Mikolas stopped beside him. "Make it two."

Ted sighed. "Saw the old guy having a few words with you."

"Yeah." Mikolas turned around to watch Trinity and leaned back against the bar as he swirled the ice in his glass. "He thinks Kronos will be back, and we need to be ready."

"Shit." Ted ran a hand down his face. "Let me guess... Zack isn't going to lose the disguise and become the all-powerful Zeus."

"I have no idea, but we can't count on him." He glanced at Ted. "The explosion on the Oceanus rig cracked Tartarus. There's a chance Kronos won't be the only one coming back for a visit."

"You're kidding me. He seriously expects us to face

off with the Father of the Gods *and* his Titan brothers?" Ted shook his head, the buzz of the alcohol fading as panic churned in his gut. His instinct to run clawed its way forward, but seriously, where could he go that a god couldn't' find him? Shit. Desperation filled his voice. "Maybe Rhea has another magic crystal or something we can use."

"Maybe. We'll have to go see her soon." Mikolas cursed under his breath, frowning as he rubbed his lower back. "Shit. Something's wrong." He snapped his head up, all his attention on Trinity.

Ted's eyes darted from Trinity to Mikolas. "What is it?"

"The mark. It's burning again." Mikolas's eyes widened. "We may not have enough time to find Rhea."

CHAPTER 2

TRINITY FINISHED HER set and placed her guitar into its fur-lined case. Zack Vrontios—Zeus disguised as a mortal—had been here tonight, and instead of speaking to her, he'd been chatting it up with Mikolas. Not that she had been watching them, not really.

But the Greek did look amazing in a tux.

She shut down the thoughts and flipped the latches closed on the case. The metallic sound echoed through the room. The sudden silence raised goosebumps on her arms as she lifted her head. Everyone in the observatory was still, frozen in time.

Her pulse raced, adrenaline pumping into her bloodstream. Kronos. It had to be. The Father of the Gods was also the God of Time itself. She'd been the victim of his time manipulations before.

So why was she still able to move?

She straightened up just in time to be caught by the waist and dragged away from her stool in the center of the room to the edge of the space in the shadows behind the crowd of immobile attendees. Before she could scream, a hand clamped over her mouth. She stared up into the dark eyes of Mikolas, the Greek billionaire who, very recently, had been the leader of the Order of the Titans. The man had almost killed her once already.

She bit his hand.

He yanked it away, growling under his breath. "Kronos is close by."

She balled her hands into fists. But if he wanted to hurt her, why hide her from Kronos? She peered through the people and whispered. "How come we can move?"

"I'm not sure." He scanned the room. "But we need to get the hell out of here."

"Not yet." It was a little surreal to be talking like this with him. He was the leader of the Order, the fanatics who nearly burned her alive. There wasn't time to worry about it right now. "I have to get Erica and the others out. I'm not leaving them here."

He shook his head. "We can't help them until we have a way to stop Kronos."

Her eyes narrowed. "There is no 'we.' Just go. I don't need your help."

He tugged up the bottom of his tux jacket and untucked his shirt. Then he pulled the waistband of his pants down a little, exposing a bright-red crescent-shaped birthmark on his hip.

Oh shit.

Mikolas Leandros was a Guardian. And she was…the only one without…

Oh gods.

She blinked, speechless for a second as she struggled to string words together. "You're a... You can't be. You were the leader of the Order. You killed Polly and ran over Lia's Guardian, Cooper, with your car. You—"

"I don't have time to explain myself now," Mikolas interrupted. You're in danger, and I don't have the crystal to banish Kronos this time. I don't even know if it would work again. We need to go. Now."

She widened her stance, bracing herself. "Not without Erica, Lia, and Cooper." She pointed across the room. "I see them right over there." Like the rest of the gala attendees, they didn't move or blink. Time stood still around them.

"We won't be able to move them," he countered.

"Then we'll carry them out. I'm not leaving them here to be tortured until Zeus decides to drop his disguise. Either help me or get out of my way."

She shoved past him, moving through the eerily still crowd of people. They would've looked like mannequins if it weren't for the fear in their eyes. Mikolas followed her, his footsteps echoing through the large observatory.

Trinity grabbed Erica's shoulders, gently shaking her. "Erica? Can you move? We've got to get out of here."

Nothing. But her eyes made it clear she was aware. Kronos had slowed time so exponentially that taking a single footstep could take hours. That was time they didn't have.

Trinity looked over at Mikolas. He was with Lia and her Guardian, Cooper. She'd half expected Mikolas to have left to save his own skin.

She wrapped her arms around Erica's waist and sucked in a deep breath as she bent her knees and lifted. She managed about five steps before she had to put Erica down. Dammit. They'd never get out fast enough.

"Trinity?"

Her head snapped in the direction of Lia's voice as she frowned. "You can move?"

"It seems so." Lia shrugged. "Mikolas and Cooper snapped me out of it somehow."

"We can figure out the details later." Mikolas grabbed Cooper's arm. "Help me break Erica out of the spell."

Cooper was Lia's Guardian. Finding her awakened a healing power inside him and a strong connection to the God, Apollo. Healing someone took a physical toll on Cooper, but he could perform miracles. They'd all witnessed it.

Mikolas gripped Cooper's shoulder. "Touch Erica."

Cooper frowned, but he did as Mikolas instructed and took her hand. Erica groaned, stumbling forward. "How did you...?"

"No time to talk." Mikolas pointed to the hallway labeled *Authorized Personnel Only*. "We need to get out of here. There's an employee exit at the end of this corridor."

Cooper and Lia ran down the hall while Trinity grabbed Erica with one hand and her guitar with the other. Mikolas brought up the rear as the front doors of the Observatory blew open on the other side of the main room.

"Run. Don't look back," Mikolas growled.

Trinity and Erica kept going until they burst through the back door into the employee parking lot. The cool autumn breeze stung her cheeks, snapping her out of the panic.

Trinity hesitated. Mikolas had the Guardian's mark; it had burned because she was in danger. The gods had chosen him to protect her.

Zeus must've been nuts. It made no sense. After Ted's father died, Mikolas had become the leader of the Order of the Titans. Mikolas could even have been the one to give the command to lock her and her sisters inside the theater while the Order set it on fire. So how was *he* her Guardian? She didn't have the answer, but she did know that the day Kronos came for them, Mikolas had stopped him and saved them all. None of it added up, but she'd never learn the truth if he waltzed back into the Observatory and got himself killed.

Trinity glanced at the door, and Erica grabbed her elbow. "Let's get out of here."

"Mikolas went back." Trinity couldn't pull her gaze away from the Observatory.

Erica squeezed her arm. "We need to warn the others that Kronos is loose."

"You don't need me for that. Go. I'll be right behind you." The words were out before she knew what she was saying. Was she seriously considering going back in that building? If she didn't, Mikolas could die alone. All those people could die. But they didn't have to. She could save them by giving Kronos the one thing he wanted most.

A daughter of Zeus.

She jerked free of Erica's grasp and handed her the guitar. "Warn Callie and the others. And keep my guitar safe. Go!"

Trinity spun around and ran back inside the Observatory.

Mikolas crept along the back wall of the circular building, ducking low as he wove though the mass of frozen people. He needed to keep the God of Time distracted to give Trinity and her friends a chance to escape. The farther away from the building they got, the better their odds of living long enough to gather their Guardians. It was Trinity's best chance to stay alive.

Kronos was back in his human form—a tall, distinguished businessman named Kevin Elys. He strode to the center of the room and perched on the stool where Trinity had been playing. Behind him, another man stepped into the light. He was taller than Kevin, but his face was hidden under a hooded black cloak. In one big, gloved hand, he carried a large spear.

Kevin chuckled, the deep sound echoing through the Observatory as he gestured to the immobile partygoers surrounding the round room. "Behold, dear Brother, my son's precious humanity."

Mikolas thought back, trying to determine who this mysterious cloaked figure was. He had been raised on stories of gods, goddesses, and Titans back home in Greece, and he knew that Kronos had five brothers. But only one had a spear at his side at all times—Iapetus. He was the Titan of Mortality, the Piercer. He'd been banished to Tartarus by Zeus and the Olympians eons ago. Yet here he was. Zack had been right. The prison was no longer able to contain them.

Fuck.

Mikolas carefully made his way through the crowd, sticking to the shadows until he neared Ted.

"I will destroy them," Iapetus's deep voice rumbled. "Then I will free Atlas. My son has been burdened by carrying this world on his shoulders for a millennium in servitude to Zeus. No more!" he bellowed.

Kevin patted his brother's shoulder. "If you truly wish to avenge your son, you must first punish Zeus as you have been. Sacrifice his precious daughters." The hood turned toward Kevin as he went on. "Yes, Brother. The muses are here in this world, and they're mortal, trapped inside human bodies."

"I will drink their life force and enjoy their father's tears." Iapetus nodded. "Zeus was never worthy of being your son. He wasn't even fit to be your cupbearer, Brother." He grunted. "Without his Olympians to protect him, we can chain your traitorous son to the depths of Tartarus. He will know our pain."

Mikolas gripped Ted's arm, but nothing happened. Shit. Without Cooper's healing power, he couldn't focus. Or something? He didn't understand how any of this worked. Earlier, when he'd sensed Kronos approaching, he'd envisioned his energy shielding Trinity. When he and Trinity were the only ones immune to Kronos's magic, he assumed his Guardian power had blocked the God of Time's magic.

But it wasn't working on Ted. Lia and Erica had awakened with Cooper's help. Maybe it only worked on Trinity because she was Mikolas's muse?

The other two muses had been awakened by Cooper's healing power. Mikolas had somehow…magnified it. Zack had called harnessing divine power. But there was nothing to harness here. No healing power without Cooper.

Dammit. What was the use of being a demigod if he didn't understand how his power worked? Or even knew what it really was…

He took out his phone and sent Ted a text. If Mikolas died tonight, he needed Ted to do something for him.

I'm going after Kronos. If I'm dead by the time you read this, protect Trinity, whether she likes it or not.

Mikolas tucked his cell back in his pocket and eyed the immortals.

"I can handle my son, but first…" Kevin waved a hand toward the immobile people. "First, you should feed, Brother. It has been far too long since you tasted mortality."

Iapetus strode forward with his spear raised. In an instant, he spun, his movements supernaturally fast. Two heads dropped to the floor with wet thuds. A moment later, the bodies they once belonged to crumpled beside them.

Mikolas's heart thundered in his ears. Demigod or not, he wouldn't last long in a physical fight with two Titans. But he had to do something.

Iapetus sucked in a long, slow breath, his chest expanding as he straightened to his full height. His form seemed even larger now, if that was possible. "I'd forgotten the sweet scent of mortality, of their fragile lifeforce teasing my nostrils."

"Okay, dude. *No one* talks like that." Trinity came into the light and stopped in front of the Titans, a hand on her hip. Being fearless and flippant was a great way to get herself killed. What was she doing?

Kevin grinned. "I remember you."

"Yeah, and I'm guessing you still want to lure Zeus into the open so you can get even." She gestured to the men and women stuck in time. "Killing these people won't do that. But I know what will. So let them go, and I'm all yours."

"No fucking way." Mikolas shouted as he came forward, every muscle in his body juiced up on adrenaline as he faced the two Titans. "Trinity, get the hell out of here."

Kevin sobered, rubbing his chin. "Why is time still moving for you two?"

The last time Mikolas had seen Kevin, Mikolas had attacked the immortal from behind with Rhea's crystal shard, so there was a good chance the Father of the Gods wouldn't recognize him. Maybe he could use it to his advantage.

"Zeus sent me." Mikolas kept his gaze locked on Kevin. "I can take you to him, but Iapetus must lower his spear."

Kevin paused, and Mikolas held his breath. The God of Time came toward him. A bead of sweat trickled down the side of his face, and a crease marred his brow. "Time remains constant around you. What *are* you?" he asked, ignoring both Mikolas's and Trinity's offers.

"I'm Mikolas Leandros, and Zeus sent me."

Kevin crossed his arms. "That doesn't answer my question."

Mikolas started to open his mouth, but sirens blared outside, deafening his ears. A voice boomed from a loudspeaker. "Crystal City Police Department.

Come out with your hands over your head."

Lia, Erica, and Cooper must've called the police.

Iapetus struck a fighting position while Kevin cursed under his breath, wiping the sweat from his brow, his eyes beginning to glow. He was losing his grip on his mortal disguise. He grabbed his brother's arm, forcing him to lower his spear. "Humanity no longer battles hand-to-hand, Brother. They can attack from a distance."

Mikolas stole a glance at Trinity. She quickly looked away. At least she could still move. Whatever demigod power he possessed, the connection between them as muse and Guardian must've kept her shielded from Kronos's time manipulation. It wasn't for a lack of trying, though. The strain on the God of Time was obvious.

Mikolas faced the immortals again. "That's a SWAT team out there. If you don't respond to their commands, they'll come inside with guns blazing."

Kronos gripped his brother's shoulder. "Come, Brother."

The air sucked out of the room, and they vanished.

Mikolas blinked. They were gone. Kronos must've sped up time to hide their retreat. It didn't matter. Mikolas didn't give a shit about Kronos right now. He ran to Trinity and grabbed her hand. She struggled for a second, but he tightened his hold.

"We need to go," he said. "Now."

They raced out the back exit and straight to his

black Mercedes. He unlocked the doors, but Trinity didn't get inside.

She crossed her arms. "I can ride back with the police."

Mikolas clenched his jaw. "Those two Titans could be anywhere. The police won't be able to protect you from them."

"But you can?" She raised a brow.

He opened the passenger door and held it for her. "You're still moving, aren't you? Unlike everyone else in the Observatory…"

She scoffed. "And you think that's because of you?"

"It's a theory." He fought the urge to throw her over his shoulder and stuff her into the passenger seat. "Look, you can be pissed at me, just let me get you away from here. It doesn't have to change anything."

She pursed her lips. "Fine."

She got in, and he slammed the door closed. As he went around to the driver's side, his hands trembled. They were far from out of the woods yet, but damn, they held their own with two Titans and they were still standing. Survival was a rush.

He drove down the delivery access road, staying away from the red flashing lights. When they were a few miles away, he finally glanced over at his silent passenger. "I told you to run away and not to look back."

"So." She stared out her window. "I saw the mark, and I'm the last muse without a Guardian so I can connect the dots, but we should get something straight right now. You may be my Guardian, but I don't trust you, and I don't answer to you."

He focused on the street. "You make it tough to protect you when you put yourself in the line of fire."

She turned his way, and he could almost feel the heat of her glare on his skin. "I was trying to save all those people. He wants a muse; I'm the best choice."

"Seriously?" He stopped at the light and let go of the wheel in exasperation. "How do you figure that?"

She looked away again. "My sisters are all in relationships, and two of them have kids. People depend on them."

He raised a brow. "Are you saying you're expendable because you're single?" The light changed, and he eased through the intersection.

She shrugged. "We were lucky to stop Kronos the first time. If we can't defeat him this time, the best hope we have to minimize the casualties is to give him what he wants."

He tightened his grip on the wheel. "Did it ever occur to you that if you discussed it with the other muses and Guardians, there might be another option?"

"I'm not an idiot." Her words were tight and clipped. "It *occurred* to me, but there wasn't time. I had to do something. And it still wasn't enough. Two people are already dead."

"It could have been much worse." Gods, she was stubborn. He decided to drop it for now. "Where am I taking you? You shouldn't be alone until we figure out what Kevin and his brother are planning."

"I live with Clio and Mason, but I don't want to go there. Not yet." She chuffed, glancing out the passenger window. "It's like I'm the eternal third wheel, but they're both too sweet to complain."

"In that case, I think I know just the place."

Trinity sent a text to Erica to let her know she was safe while he navigated the dark streets. When he turned into the parking lot of the soon-to-be-opened *Les Neuf Soeurs* theater, he caught a rare curve to her lips.

She glanced his way. "I'm surprised."

"How so?" He parked and turned off the engine and headlights.

"Just wouldn't expect you to return to the scene of the crime."

And there it was again. Her distaste for him was palpable.

He ran a hand down his face. "I'm well aware that you don't believe me, but I didn't know about the fire until I saw the coverage on the news."

"Bullshit." She got out of the car and slammed the door, walking toward the theater.

He slapped his hand against the steering wheel, but there wasn't time to cool off. He couldn't let her wander into the darkness alone. Kronos and Iapetus could be anywhere.

Mikolas followed behind her, taking a good long

look at the theater the muses had sacrificed so much to see open. The building itself was a work of art with nine sides, each one with a rendering of a Greek muse. Visitors would admire the Theater of the Muses, and never guess the muses were still alive inside each of the women on the board of directors.

He stopped behind Trinity while she unlocked the glass doors. She glanced back at him. "Mason and the guys did an incredible job on this place. Thanks to Ted, we couldn't get a single general contractor to work with us."

"I didn't—"

"I know." She put a hand up as she interrupted. "Ted started blackballing this theater long before you landed in Crystal City." She pointed to the vaulted ceiling of the lobby. "This was Clio's idea. It's a memorial to Nia and Polly."

She flipped a switch, and scrolls suspended in midair were illuminated by myriad tiny lights twinkling in the darkness. Some of the scrolls were unrolled, exposing the pages of music and familiar lyrics. He squinted, bringing them into focus. Hymns. Hundreds of them. The small bulbs only illumined a few words here and there, but the effect sent a ripple of energy through him—inspiration.

Mikolas couldn't take his eyes off it. "For Polyhymnia and Urania... It's perfect." He met her eyes. "My grandmother was her generation's Urania." He hadn't expected the words to fall from his lips, but he couldn't pull them back now. "My grandfather waited until I was thirteen to explain what my birthmark meant. I assumed I would be the Guardian for my generation's Urania…"

Understanding clicked in her expression. "That's why you donated the giant telescope in Nia's memory."

He nodded and glanced back up at the ceiling. "When I discovered the Order had killed her…" He shook his head, casting his gaze to the floor. "I'd been marked by the gods to be her protector. It was my purpose from birth, and I failed." He lifted his eyes to meet hers. "But when I found you that day when Kronos attacked after the dance recital, the mark burned, and I knew."

Trinity stared up at him, her voice barely a whisper. "*I'm* your muse."

"Yes." It took all his self-control not to touch her. He'd been marked for her as the ancient prophecy foretold. The mystical connection between them tugged at him, but the reality was, he barely knew her, and she seemed content to loathe his existence.

She was his muse, and he'd defended her from Kronos twice already. But she was hardly "his," not even close. He swallowed the lump that was creeping up his throat. "I'll fight until my last breath to protect you."

"No." She broke eye contact and went to the ornately carved interior double doors leading to the main theater. "There's enough blood on my hands already. I don't want yours, too."

CHAPTER 3

TED WOKE UP in a hospital bed. Though *woke* wasn't really the right word. He'd been awake for what seemed like lifetimes. But he could finally move. He was no longer trapped in a Titan-induced time warp. Ted had witnessed Kronos's time manipulations on others before, but this was the first time he'd been caught in it.

When time ceased to exist, when it stopped, he couldn't find words to describe the wasteland. He could witness the world, but not react. He shuddered pushing the memories away.

Kronos hadn't been alone this time. He'd had a partner with him.

Brother.

A monitor started to buzz, and a nurse came rushing in. She checked the screens with an empathetic smile. "Welcome back, Mr. Belkin."

"Mr. Belkin was my dad. You can call me Ted." He glanced around the room and rubbed his forehead with his free hand. "How long have I been—" *Stuck?* "—immobile?"

"About two hours." She punched some numbers

into her tablet and then met his eyes.

Ted frowned. "What happened to everyone else?"

"From the Observatory?" She glanced at her tablet again. "We received eight patients from the gala; the rest were transported to Mercy and Crystal City General." She lifted her gaze. "Did you have a family member with you?"

"No. Just friends."

She nodded and glanced at the door. "There's a detective here. Maybe he can check on your friends."

Speak of the devil…

Detective Nate Malone filled the doorway. He smiled at the nurse. "Mind if I ask Mr. Belkin some questions?"

"Sure. But don't be too long. His vitals are stable, but the doctor is coming by soon to look him over."

Malone nodded his thanks and entered the room so she could pass through the door. He approached the bed, his old-school notepad and pen in hand. Nate Malone was the first Guardian to emerge in Crystal City. Since then, he'd married his muse, Mel, the Muse of Tragic Poetry. And because Ted had given the order to have Mel abducted two years ago, his relationship with Detective Malone was dicey at best. Luckily, the detective was a true law-and-order man. He wouldn't kill Ted, but if he had the chance to lock him in a jail cell and throw away the key, Ted had no doubt Malone would take it.

The detective cleared his throat, keeping his voice

hushed. "Did Kronos see you at the Observatory tonight?"

"I don't think so." Ted frowned. "Why?"

Nate set the notepad on the bed. "Because Trinity told us Kronos isn't alone this time, and we need a man on the inside if we're going to get ahead of this. Two people died tonight, and more will follow if we don't anticipate his movements."

The machines monitoring Ted's pulse beeped faster. Fear twisted in his gut, the memory of being trapped in his own body while Kronos's brother beheaded two people flashed through his mind. And as much as he wanted to help Trinity, to be a hero for her…he didn't have it in him.

He shook his head, relieved and ashamed at the same time with his decision. "This isn't my problem. I helped trap Kronos once already. My debt is paid." Ted shifted in the hospital bed, scooting up farther, hoping his expression looked more determined than it felt.

Nate leaned in closer, gripping the railing of the bed until the color drained from his knuckles. "Unless you can bring Nia and Polly back from the dead, you still owe us plenty." He straightened up, shaking his head. "If that's not enough to convince you, don't forget that Trinity won't be safe until we figure out a way to stop these Titans."

Ted's gut twisted. "Even if I wanted to be your mole with Kronos, it's not like I can just text him. How do you expect me to get close?"

"Make yourself available." Malone rolled his shoulders back. "Our only advantage is that Kronos and his brother are strangers in this world. They don't understand the technology. They're going to need you. Kevin knows where you work. He'll find you."

"They." Ted corrected. "He wasn't alone this time. He brought his brother out of Tartarus."

"Yeah." Malone picked up his notepad. "Trinity said it was Iapetus, the Piercer."

Ted squirmed, running a hand down his face. "Shit."

"Exactly." He slipped the notepad into his pocket and met Ted's eyes. "Hunter's going to help me stake out Belkin Oil. We'll have eyes on you the whole time."

Hunter Armstrong was a retired Navy SEAL, but even with his weapons training and physical stamina, Iapetus was a force of nature—the God of Mortality. They were fucked. The legends claimed he moved with impossible speed, killing before a mortal eye ever caught sight of him.

But there weren't many options. It wasn't like there was anywhere to hide. These were immortal beings, born of Mother Earth herself, children of Gaia.

"Okay." Ted nodded, wishing he had a better choice. "When they let me out of here, I'll go to my office."

"Good." Malone patted the railing on the hospital bed. "Keep me informed once you know what they're planning."

Malone left the room, and Ted kicked his feet off the bed. This was nuts. He should get the hell out of Dodge. But where could he run that the titans couldn't find him? He stood up and scanned the room for his clothes. A bag labeled PERSONAL BELONGINGS sat on a chair across the room. He wandered over and dug through his things for his cell phone.

When he found it, a text from Mikolas was waiting for him:

Protect Trinity.

Ted frowned, sorting through the memories. Mikolas had been there with Trinity. He had warned Kevin about the police outside. Iapetus had swung his spear. Two bodies had fallen, but Ted hadn't been able to move to see who they were.

Was Mikolas dead?

There was only one way to find out. He fired off a quick text:

Did you make it out?

He tossed his phone on the bed and took out his clothes. Screw the doctor releasing him. He was leaving.

Now.

Trinity walked down the aisle of the theater, trying to control the crescendo of emotions Mikolas was churning up inside her. This entire place was built on blood, sweat, and far too many tears. They'd fought through soul-crushing losses, but she and her muse sisters struggled to keep pushing forward, inspired by the ones they'd lost.

And now the grand opening was only two weeks away.

Or at least it had been before the Father of the Gods showed up with his spear-wielding brother. Tonight, the Titans had claimed the lives of two innocent people. A couple of years ago, the gore of blood and bodies would've left her in shock, but a sick numbness filled the cracks in her heart now.

She climbed the stairs on the side of the stage. Mikolas stood in the house, his hands in the pockets of his disheveled tuxedo. His bow tie was gone, and the top two buttons were open on his shirt. And he was still so damned beautiful.

Her vision wavered as she blinked back unwelcome tears. She sat down on the edge of the stage, resting her hands on either side of her body. She stared up at the balcony seats. "We fought so hard to build this place because we truly believed that inspiration could change the world." She shook her head, dropping her gaze to her feet. "I'm not going to let all that sacrifice be for nothing. As long as I'm breathing, we're opening this theater."

Mikolas came closer to the stage, his deep voice resonating with the natural acoustics of the theater. "My grandmother never found her muse sisters, but she had dreams about this theater. When I was a boy, she'd tell me about the daughters of Zeus who had the most important burden to carry for the future."

Trinity lifted her head. "How could you know all that and still get mixed up with the Order of the Titans?"

"Long story." He ran his fingers through his dark hair. There was no taming the wavy curls. His eyes locked on hers. "My grandfather encouraged my father to join the original Order back home in Greece. He thought the best way to keep the muses safe was to know what the enemy had planned. My father rose through the ranks of the Order, and eventually he learned about the progress of the Order in Crystal City. Ted Belkin, Sr. owned an oil company with an offshore rig with a mission that had nothing to do with oil. We had to stop them. But we were too late."

"The Oceanus rig." Trinity crossed her arms. "Ted's father cracked into the Earth's core before he died. He blamed the explosion on an equipment failure."

"Right. But he had told the international chapters of the Order of the Titans that the rise of Kronos was imminent." Mikolas took a couple of steps closer to the stage. "My father and grandfather had invested heavily in Belkin Oil so they could position me to infiltrate the

America Order."

She raised a brow. "You were a spy."

"Not exactly. We didn't expect Ted Belkin, Sr. to die, but we owned enough of the stock to push the board toward proclaiming me CEO. At the time, I was eager to get here. I thought my life's calling to be the Guardian of the Muse of Astronomy was in sight…" His gaze fell to the floor. "But by the time I arrived in Crystal City, Nia was already dead, and the Order had trained an enforcer to go after more muses." He lifted his head. "I know you probably don't believe a word I'm saying, but I need you to know that I didn't order anyone to burn down this theater. And I wasn't behind the wheel of my car when Cooper was hit, either. I forbade all of it."

Part of her actually believed him. Gods, would she never learn? Her taste in men was deadly. How many friends would she have to lose before she accepted that reality?

"Why are you telling me all this?" she asked.

He came all the way forward, but with her being seated up on the stage, he still had to look up her. There was no trace of hesitation in his voice. "Because I want you to know you can trust me."

Cynical laughter escaped her lips as she rolled her eyes. His gaze didn't falter, and the intensity in his dark eyes shook her. She focused on her shoes instead. "Has Ted ever told you about us?"

"I know you two dated."

She got to her feet and wandered to the center of the stage before risking a glance in his direction. "Maybe that's all it was to him." Her self-loathing roared like a hungry lion in her soul. "I loved that asshole. Gods, I was so blind. I trusted him and shared the dreams about Euterpe that started haunting me. Eventually, I started to think I needed to go to Crystal City, and Ted made me believe I wasn't a freak."

She cursed under her breath. Talking about it out loud left her feeling vulnerable and weak. She'd promised herself a million times she'd never do it again, yet here she was confiding in another man.

"I trusted the wrong guy, and it cost two of my friends their lives." Her voice faded as she spoke, but she meant every word. "I refuse to lose anyone else."

THE PAIN IN Trinity's eyes tore into Mikolas. Ted had shared his side of the story, but hearing Trinity blame herself and witnessing the aftermath of Ted's betrayal made Mikolas ache to beat the shit out of Ted. Trinity got up and walked farther upstage.

Mikolas jogged up the steps and followed her into the shadows. "Trinity, wait."

She sighed and stopped. Slowly, she turned to face him. "What?"

"It's not your fault."

"Bullshit." She stared up at him, scanning his face

and pressing her lips together. "If I'd never confided in Ted, Nia and Polly would be alive. His father would have never known they were muses. They followed me to Crystal City, and I led them right to my sisters."

"What if you and your sisters aren't the end game here? When I went to meet with Rhea at Blessed Mary's Village and she showed me the shard containing a piece of one of Zeus's lightning bolts, it occurred to me that there is more happening here in Crystal City than just the opening of the *Les Neuf Soeurs* theater."

A crease formed on her forehead. "How do you figure that?"

"You and your muse sisters had dreams that led you to this city, to a rundown theater with potential, right?"

She nodded slowly.

"So why was Rhea already hiding in Crystal City?" He paused, letting his words sink in. "And she's not alone. Her elderly poker group friends Mrs. Mardas and Mrs. Spanos are really Titias and Kyllenos, the Guiders of Destiny. I can't believe that is coincidence."

She searched his eyes. "And Zeus is here, too."

"This is bigger than you and your sisters." Mikolas slid his hand in his pocket. "I think the Guiders of Destiny saw this turning point coming."

"They knew Tartarus wouldn't hold Kronos forever."

"That's my guess," he agreed. "And to take it a step further, I'd guess that Zeus sent his daughters of this generation those dreams because this theater is going to be a beacon of inspiration for humanity. And we're going to need it if we're faced with doing battle against the Titans. None of this is random."

"But we can't win." Trinity shook her head. "We're mortal. Even the Guardians. You each have a gift, but none of you are strong enough to face a Titan."

"Zeus told me he would handle his father. Maybe with the help of the other Guardians we can stop Iapetus. The muses and Guardians stopped Philyra. Maybe we can do it again."

Trinity stared at the floor. "There is no *we*, Mikolas." She sighed and looked up at him again. "I want to believe you, which makes me even more wary of trusting you. My instincts suck when it comes to men. Besides, after everything we've been through with the Order, none of the muses and Guardians are going to be excited to see you."

All true, but dammit, he wasn't going to walk away. He reached for her hand and she didn't pull away. It seemed so small in his. He met her eyes, his voice softening. "You don't have to trust me. You don't even need to like me. But Zeus chose me to be your Guardian for a reason we probably don't understand yet. Finding you awakened something inside me, and if I can use that gift to keep you safe, then it's worth figuring out how it works. Help me learn to control it. I'm not expecting anything more from you."

A sad smile curved her lips. "You can't possibly be

that selfless."

He chuckled. Trinity didn't mince words, but the honesty was refreshing. He'd grown up as the only son in a wealthy family. He'd experienced more than his share of women who would've told him anything in hopes of gaining a piece of his inheritance. A woman pushing him away was new.

"I'm far from selfless." He drank in her dark eyes with their flecks of gold. One of a kind. Just like she was. "But I've waited my entire life to find you, and I'll protect you, or die trying." He had whispered the words before he'd even realized he was going to speak.

She withdrew her hand. "Okay, I bet that romantic crap has women all over the world throwing their panties at you." Regret flashed in her eyes. "But I'm not going to be another conquest."

He ached to touch her again, but she was right about one thing. Trinity Porter wasn't a conquest; she was far more precious. He looked out at the empty seats. "Destiny is playing out in Crystal City. This generation will decide the future of mankind." Facing her again, he almost smiled. "You're going to change the world."

"We have to live long enough first."

"That's where I come in." He dusted off the sleeves of his tux, hoping the goofy gesture might coax a smile from her. "Zack told me finding you made me a demigod."

The sound of her laughter inspired a symphony of

emotions inside him. For the first time, she looked up at him not with disdain but with a playful smirk. "Wow. So you're Achilles now?"

He shook his head. "I think I'm more a channel for energy. Or maybe I magnify it? Hell if I know. I was hoping my muse might help me hone it before we face Kronos and his brother again."

He hadn't meant to claim her as his, but the words were out of his mouth now. He couldn't reel them back.

Trinity stiffened, her smile fading. "There's still no *we* between us." She paused and added, "But you can call me Trin. And I guess I don't hate you anymore."

Baby steps.

He nodded slowly. "Progress."

His phone buzzed in his pocket. He frowned, taking it out. A text from Ted lit up the screen. Mikolas lifted his gaze to her face. "The guests from the gala at the Observatory are awake."

CHAPTER 4

TED STEPPED OFF the elevator in the Belkin Oil highrise. His assistant, Marion, greeted him as she had for years, like nothing had changed. He stopped near her desk, refusing to take even this small gesture for granted.

"It's good to see you, too, Marion."

The wrinkles around her eyes deepened as she grinned. "Thank you. Let me know if I can get you anything."

"Will do." He walked away, making a mental note that if they somehow figured out a way to save the human race from the Titans, he needed to gift some stock to Marion. She'd worked for Belkin longer than Ted had been alive, and for most of that time, she'd been supporting assholes like him and his father, but she never complained.

He sat behind his desk, glancing at his e-mails and trying to muster some concern for business as usual. It all seemed pointless. Two Titans were in Crystal City. What did property rights on oil pumping equipment matter at this point?

While he'd been trapped inside of Kronos's time

warp, the Titans hadn't destroyed the world. At least not yet. He had no idea if Detective Malone's plan would work, though. Would the Titans really show up here looking for Ted's help? Half of him hoped not; he'd be thrilled if he never had to look at Kevin Elys again.

But if he could get on the inside, he might have a chance to keep Trinity from becoming a casualty of this battle of immortals.

"Excuse me, Ted?" Marion poked her head in the door.

Every muscle in his body tensed. He thought he'd have more time. "Yes?"

"I just wanted to make sure you're all right. The attack at the gala last night has been all over the news." Concern lined her face. "Are you sure you don't need to be home resting? I can reschedule meetings and take messages."

Shit, he didn't deserve her concern. In the years before his father had died, he'd taken frustrations out on Marion, but in spite of his poor treatment, here she was, worried about him. Did the universe have to remind him over and over what an asshole he was?

"I'm fine." He cleared his throat. "You don't need to worry about me. The police think there must've been some kind of gas leak or something. I don't remember very much."

"Did you know Mr. and Mrs. Enright?"

"Yes." He frowned. "Why?"

Her eyes widened. "You didn't know? Oh, I shouldn't have—"

"Wait. Are they the two who were killed last night?" The news threw him for a loop. The Enright's had been big donors to many social organizations in Crystal City. Ted's father had entertained them many times. They were kind people. And now they were dead because he'd been naive enough to believe freeing the Titans would save the world. Guilt tightened his chest.

"I'm so sorry." Marion shook her head.

"No." He swallowed the lump in his throat. "I'm glad you told me." He rubbed his forehead. "Can you do me a favor?"

"Anything." She offered a sympathetic smile.

"Take the rest of the day off."

She frowned. "But it's only ten in the morning."

The last thing he wanted was for Marion to be another casualty in this battle between Zeus and Kronos. "Please. Take a day with pay. I'll be leaving early anyway."

"Well…" She paused. "If you're sure."

"I'm certain. I'll see you tomorrow."

If there is one.

MIKOLAS PARKED ON Lothlórien Lane across the street from Callie O'Connor's home. He'd never been there before, but the address was well-known to the Order of the Titans. The group had been staking out her house before Mikolas had even arrived in Crystal City.

Callie was the vessel for the Muse of Epic Poetry and acted as the leader of the muses. He hadn't imagined he'd ever be walking through her door. He'd come to Crystal City as the new leader of the Order after Ted's father died of a heart attack, and although Mikolas had an agenda to keep the muses safe, at the time, he couldn't let them know without blowing his cover.

Trinity was already there, explaining his situation, so with any luck, he wouldn't be shot on sight. Although with his new status as a demigod, maybe he could survive a bullet. He wasn't sure how it all worked yet.

A big guy at the front door narrowed his eyes as Mikolas approached. Mikolas recognized him. The day he had banished Kronos to Tartarus, this man had been the only person able to move.

Mikolas offered his hand. "I'm Mikolas Leandros."

"Gavin" He gave him a firm handshake. "I'm Tera's Guardian. Trinity told us to expect you."

"I remember you from the dance recital. You were the only one who could move when Kronos stopped time for the others."

"Yeah." His posture remained stiff and defensive. "My gift is speed, so apparently his time manipulations don't work right on me. If Tera's in danger, I'm supersonic."

He'd suspected it before. Maybe that was part of the reason he couldn't break the spell over Ted at the Observatory. "Our ability is connected to our muse being in danger?"

"Yeah. Nate figured it out. His power doesn't kick in unless Mel is threatened. Maybe it's Zeus's way of keeping us from becoming superheroes? Who knows."

Another man came out the door and plowed into Mikolas, knocking him back a few steps. "I don't give a *fuck* if you convinced Trinity that you're her Guardian. You stay the *hell* out of here."

Mikolas balled his hands into fists but managed to keep from retaliating. He recognized this guy. Reed McIntosh. He was the firefighter who almost died saving all the muses, including Trinity, from the inferno at the theater.

"I had nothing to do with the fire at *Les Neuf Soeurs*," Mikolas blurted out. Reed didn't reply. Mikolas shook his head. "I didn't even know about it until I saw the news reports."

"Bull*shit*." Reed came closer, rage burning in his eyes. "I almost lost *everything* because of the fucking Order; I'm not going to sit at a table with you and pretend you're one of the team."

A short woman with a pixie haircut jogged down the front steps and inserted herself between them. Mikolas recognized her, too. Callie O'Connor, the Muse of Epic Poetry. She was a therapist for the military, and from everything Mikolas had heard about her from Ted, she was a force to be reckoned with.

She looked up at Reed. "No one is asking you two to be best friends, but Trinity saw his birthmark. The gods chose Mikolas to protect her, and Kronos isn't alone this time. We're going to need all the help we can get."

Reed's nostrils flared, his face flushed with color. "With help like his, we may as well surrender to Kronos now before he breaks us down from the inside."

A week ago, Mikolas would have welcomed the abuse of his name and his honor, but now that he knew there was still a chance to fulfill his destiny and keep the Muse of Music safe, he was prepared to fight until his last breath if that's what it took.

"Hate me if it makes you feel better, but Zack gave me information at the Observatory gala that might help all of us." Mikolas crossed his arms. "I'm here to protect Trinity, not make friends."

Callie looked at each of them. "We've got two Titans on the loose, and our theater opens in less than two weeks. You guys can beat your chests later. For now, we need to work together."

Reed narrowed his eyes. "I'll be watching you."

Mikolas bumped his shoulder as he passed by. "Stay out of my way, and we'll be fine."

The tension inside the house was palpable, but when he entered. He passed through the living area and into the dining room. Trinity sat at a long table chatting with Erica, some of the hostility eased across his shoulders.

She lifted her head, and her gaze locked on his. "I saved you a seat."

Mikolas crossed the room, ignoring the rest of the attention. Fighting the other Guardians wasn't going to help Trinity. Her safety was more important than his pride.

She offered a tentative smile as he took the chair beside her. "I told everyone about your birthmark."

He raised a brow with a slight nod. "Yeah, I can see it went over well."

Erica bit her lower lip, clearly trying to hold back a smile. "Reed couldn't wait to meet you."

He chuckled. "That's one way to look at it." He sobered. "I'm only here to be sure Trin is performing center stage at the grand opening."

Erica grinned. "She doesn't let just anyone call her that."

"Slow down." Trinity shook her head quickly. "It's not like that. I agreed not to hate him anymore. That's it."

Which was all true. But damn, hearing it out loud sucked. He cleared his throat and nodded to Erica. "Good to see you again."

"Likewise." There was a coquettish curve to her full lips, but Mikolas knew better than to think she was actually flirting with him. Erica shared space in her soul with Erato, the Muse of Erotic Poetry and Lyrics.

She inspired passion without even trying.

He glanced at Trinity. "We can skip introductions. I think I know everyone already."

Erica nudged Trinity. "My best friend here surprised all of us when she explained your undercover plan to infiltrate the Order."

Mikolas scanned the stern faces around the room. "I can imagine."

Callie herded the muses and their Guardians to the table. She stood at the end with Hunter seated beside her. "Obviously everyone is on edge. Between Trin finding her Guardian, and Kronos bringing Iapetus back from Tartarus with him, there's plenty for us to worry about, but for now, Mikolas was the last one of us to speak to Zack, so maybe he can bring us up to speed." Her gaze landed on Mikolas. "Well?"

Mikolas was accustomed to tense board meetings, but between Reed shooting daggers with his eyes and the carpenter, Mason looking ready to jump across the table at the slightest provocation, this was over the top.

He started to open his mouth, but Trinity beat him to it. "Guys, if Mikolas meant us harm, he had plenty of chances to kill me last night and he didn't. And his power kept Kronos from being able to stop time on me."

Cooper cleared his throat. "He kept Trinity from being affected by Kronos's magic, and he snapped me out of it too. I'm not sure how to explain it, but when he gripped my shoulder, he channeled my healing power somehow. When I touched Lia and Erica, the spell was broken too. I'm not sure how to explain it." He looked over at Reed. "We only got out of that observatory last night because Mikolas helped us."

"Question is, why is he helping us now?" Reed crossed his arms. "What's in it for him?"

Fuck this shit.

Mikolas stood up. "If I could change the past I would. Trust me. I wish I could've gotten here sooner before the Order got violent with you. But that wasn't how it played out, and if we want to live long enough to see that theater open, you're going to have to cut me a break."

He waited, his gaze slowly crossing each member around the table except for Reed. The firefighter refused eye contact, but he didn't tell Mikolas to fuck off, so that was a small improvement. He sat down beside Trinity and brought them up to speed on what Zack had told them at the Observatory: Zeus would handle Kronos, but Iapetus would need to be stopped.

Mason glanced at Clio, the Muse of History, before he met Mikolas's eyes. "My gift is Herculean strength, but I'm also a Lycan. That's how we killed Philyra, even though she was immortal. My family line was cursed by Zeus. When I shift into a wolf, his magic makes me immune to their powers, and if Clio is in danger, my strength kicks in."

Mikolas raised a brow. "You were strong enough to finish off an immortal?"

"The wolf decapitated her." Mason shifted in his chair. "I think the combo of the strength and Zeus's magic when I was in my Lycan form made it possible."

"Maybe we can play out the same scenario with Iapetus," Mikolas pondered aloud.

"No." Callie waved her hands and stood up. "No way. Again, our goal, *our mission*, is to inspire humanity, not hunt immortals. We can die. They can't." She scanned each person at the long table. "Philyra was not a Titan, and she gave us no choice." She turned toward Mikolas. "So we don't fight Iapetus unless we absolutely have to. This is Zeus's battle, not ours. We have to stay focused on *our* purpose."

Mikolas nodded, and Callie moved on to organizing the final touches for the grand opening of the *Les Neuf Soeurs* theater.

While he understood Callie's hesitation to face off with a Titan, he also knew the legends about Iapetus. Hiding from the God of Mortality was wishful thinking, as impossible as cheating death itself. He would come for them, and they needed to be ready.

He stared across the table at Mason. The Lycan had already slain an immortal. It was possible. They just needed a solid plan.

CHAPTER 5

The Belkin Oil offices emptied at five o'clock, leaving Ted on his own. He stood at the window and stared down at the parking lot below. Kevin had never showed. Maybe the Titans didn't need him after all.

He should be relieved, but a sick pit was forming in his stomach. What if there was no containing this? Then mankind really was perched on the edge of the apocalypse.

From his earliest memories, his father had raised him to believe that the mission to free Kronos from Tartarus would *save* the world, not end it. No more wars, no famine, only days of milk and honey. The Titans were supposed to protect mankind. Part of his brain still couldn't comprehend this warped reality he was witnessing. The Golden Age of Man wasn't returning. Instead, they were facing the end of humanity.

Someone knocked on the door. Ted jumped, spinning around.

Kevin Elys stood in the doorway with a smirk. "Surprised to see me again, Ted?"

The Father of the Gods wore a well-cut, gun-smoke

gray business suit with polished black wingtip shoes. His silver hair was slicked back, as if he'd just come from a business meeting instead of a double homicide at the Observatory.

Ted struggled to compose himself. "I wondered if you would come."

Kevin stepped back to allow another man to enter the office. "This is my brother, Iapetus. We need your help."

Iapetus was no longer hidden underneath a hooded robe. Kevin had fitted him with an expensive black suit with a light-blue button-down shirt that matched his cold blue eyes. The florescent lighting reflected off his bald head as his hands balled into fists.

But at least there was no spear.

Ted slid his hand into his pocket. He couldn't trust it not to tremble. "What could two all-mighty Titans need from a useless mortal like me?"

Kevin chuckled. "I may have underestimated humanity last time. I won't make the same mistake twice." He sobered. "I need identification for Iapetus with an American-sounding name. Maybe Ian Elys."

Ted crossed his arms, doing his best to remain calm and cool. "Before I help you, I want assurances that whatever you have planned for humanity, I'll be spared."

"You're in no position to make deals, Ted." Kevin's eyes sparked with malice.

Ted swallowed to wet his suddenly dry throat.

"Maybe not, but you need me…and those are my terms."

Kevin glanced at Iapetus. "He understands human technology, Brother. I think we can allow this one to live."

The future Ian Elys nodded, disdain smoldering in his gaze. Even without his spear, his presence oozed foreboding and dread. "Agreed."

Relief flooded Ted's tense muscles. "Good. I can have his identification ready by tomorrow night." He moved behind his desk and sat down. "Is there anything else?"

The corner of Kevin's mouth quirked up. "Yes."

Ted lifted his eyes to the immortal's very human-looking face. "What is it?"

"I want tickets to the theater."

Ted picked up his phone. "That's not a problem. What show do you want to see?"

"You misunderstand. I want tickets to *Les Neuf Soeurs*."

Oh shit. Ted lowered his cell. "You can't walk in there. They know your name and your face. You'll never get through the door."

Kevin dropped his head back, his laughter rattling the windows of Ted's office.

Fuck. It was like an earthquake.

Ted covered his ears, his heart pounding like a jackhammer in his chest. The Titan came forward and slammed his hand down on Ted's desk, demanding his full attention.

Ted slowly uncovered his ears. "I'll do my best, but I don't think it opens until the end of next week."

"That gives us time to acclimate Iapetus—" Kevin cleared his throat "—Ian, to this world."

Ted nodded as evenly as he could when his pulse was racing faster than ever before. "All right. I'll work on the ID first, and then I can look into theater tickets." He kept his focus on Kevin. "Where are you staying?"

"I'm still renting the mansion on the hill." He turned for the door and gestured his brother to set out. But Kevin turned back. "Your business partner, Mikolas, is a Guardian. Distance yourself. I demand your full loyalty; without it, our agreement is terminated."

Iapetus was suddenly at Ted's side with a blade pressed to his neck. Fuck, the guy really was fast. Ted hadn't even seen the Titan move.

He sniffed the side of Ted's face. His voice was so deep it rumbled. "His fear is…intoxicating."

Kevin raised his hand. "Come, Brother." His gaze landed on Ted once more. "If you betray me, I won't curb my brother's appetite next time."

The immortals were gone as suddenly as they'd arrived. Ted leaned back in his chair and looked up at the ceiling. He was so screwed.

Trinity strolled the cereal aisle of the grocery store, humming the old Cheerios jingle and pretending she didn't notice all the women staring at the tall, dark, and handsome man trailing behind her. Since the meeting at Callie's, Mikolas had been quiet and withdrawn, but Trinity wasn't complaining. He was her Guardian, not her boyfriend, and last night it had been too easy to blur the lines. She grabbed a box of Honey Nut Cheerios and spun around, almost slamming right in his chest.

She looked up as she stepped back, out of his personal space. "Sorry." She pointed to the shelves. "Did you want some cereal?"

He shook his head. "No."

"Your loss." She turned, heading for the checkout and fighting the urge to coax him to talk. What was the point? It wasn't like they were even friends—just two people Zeus thought would work well together.

The song "That's Amore" bursting from his cell phone broke the silence in a big way. She glanced over at him, trying not to laugh as he hustled to answer it. But Mikolas wasn't smiling. Far from it. And he had answered the call in Greek.

She continued toward the registers, wishing she didn't find his deep voice so sexy, even when she couldn't understand a word he was saying. She peered over her shoulder and caught him looking right at her. Then she recognized her name on his lips, and her hackles rose. Why was he talking about her? She gripped the box tighter, a small dose of adrenaline lacing her bloodstream.

Shit. She'd done it again. She'd brought him into Callie's house and had given him a seat at their table.

"Trin, wait."

She spun around, her finger poking him in the middle of his chest. "You don't get to call me that anymore."

His brow shot up. "Are you mad that I don't like cereal?"

"What? No." How in the hell had he come to that conclusion? "Ever since we left the meeting at Callie's, you've been quiet and moody, and then your cell rings and next thing I know you're talking about me in Greek. I never should have trusted you. I'm an idiot."

She marched over to the self-checkout and slammed her box of Cheerios on the self-checkout while she fished her wallet out of her purse and maintained the intensity in her drop-dead glare.

Mikolas bagged her cereal and carried it out of the store for her as if she hadn't just foiled his plot. Once they were outside, she trailed behind him this time, wishing he was in one of his power suits. His Levi's fit him too well. It was distracting.

When he got to his car, he turned around and leaned against the trunk. She snatched the bag from his hand. "Are you even going to deny it?"

He ran a hand down his face. "'That's Amore' is my grandmother's favorite song."

She placed her hand on her hip. "What does that have to do with anything?"

"It was my grandmother on the phone. I told her I was with you, which was why you heard your name."

"And I'm just supposed to believe you?"

He crossed his arms. "If I had bad intentions, would I really have that ring tone for my associates? Kind of draws attention, right?"

Okay, that made sense. Dammit. She sighed. "I'm not usually such a crazy person."

He shrugged. "After your experience with Ted, I understand." His gaze locked on hers. "I'd like to earn your trust one day."

She walked past him to the passenger door. "What did your grandmother want?"

He popped the locks. "Apparently she's coming to your theater opening."

Trinity got in the car and looked over at him. "You told her we were opening soon?"

"No." He glanced over at her as he opened iTunes on his phone. "But Trinity Porter has a new single called 'Find Your Muse' that's shooting up on the charts, and my grandmother heard Trinity was performing at the grand opening of a theater in Crystal City, *Les Neuf Soeurs*. That's when she bought her plane ticket."

With all the danger swirling in the air after the gala at the Observatory, she'd forgotten all about the new song. "Callie and Erica thought I should perform 'Find your Muse' for the opening. I guess I didn't realize the name of the theater might catch the eye of muses from other generations."

"I wonder how many of them are out there."

Trinity shrugged. "I don't know." She peered over at him. "Did you tell her not to come? We can't be sure it'll be safe for muses with Kronos on the loose again."

"I tried, but my nona is a force of nature, and being a former Muse of Astronomy, she believes you will need her for the opening since Nia is gone. She says it will take all the daughters of Zeus to unleash the magic." He stared out the windshield. "She'll be here next week. My grandfather is coming with her. She acts like she's bulletproof when he's beside her."

"He's a Guardian, too?"

Mikolas nodded. "Yes. His gift is instant healing."

"Like Cooper."

He shook his head. "No. Cooper can heal others. My grandfather can't be injured. He heals rapidly."

"Like Wolverine?"

"Yes." Mikolas chuckled. "My grandfather is a seventy-nine-year-old X-Man."

She laughed, and it felt so damned good. "So you have X-Men in Greece?"

His smile made it tough to keep reminding herself that trusting another man would lead to another betrayal.

"While my grandparents filled my head with Greek gods and goddesses, I secretly read every comic book I could get my hands on." Mikolas turned her way. "What about you?"

"It was Disney for me. Before I realized I carried Euterpe in my soul, I wanted to grow up to be a voice for a Disney character. I made demos and attended auditions, but I never got a callback." Erica was the only other person who knew about Trinity's unfulfilled childhood dream, but it fell out so easily with him.

He patted her knee. "I think the universe had another plan for you."

"Maybe so." She'd never considered that angle before. Maybe her stars had always been leading her toward this moment in time. She swallowed the lump in her throat. "My car is back at my place. I rode to Callie's with Clio and Mason."

He reached for the ignition, but he didn't turn the key. "Do you agree with Callie about staying away from the Titans?"

Trinity shrugged. "What's not to agree with? We're mortals. We're not equipped to fight two Titans who can't die."

"I think we only need to face one." He glanced into the rearview mirror. "Zeus told me he'd handle his father."

Her eyes widened. "That leaves you seriously considering duking it out with the Titan who bears the catchy nickname the Piercer?" She shook her head. "We don't even know how your demigod status works. You'll get yourself killed."

"I don't think so. They wouldn't be expecting us to come for them."

"You're serious about this." Trinity frowned. "It's noble, but you can't win. This isn't our fight."

Our. Where had that come from?

She relaxed back against the headrest. "Can I ask you something?"

"Sure." He turned on the engine.

"Why are you so determined to face them?"

He pulled out of the parking space while he answered. "Because it's my destiny. Zeus tied our souls together for a reason. I'm not going to fail."

He'd called his grandmother a force of nature, but the apple didn't fall far from the tree. His stubborn devotion to his fate was going to lead him down a dark road. And somewhere deep in her stupid heart, a pang of regret blossomed. For once, she wished she could just be a girl with a boy. Being a muse had caused Ted to betray her, and now it would cost Mikolas his life.

This wasn't the kind of future she had hoped to inspire.

By the time she dug her way out of her mental funk, Mikolas was parking across the street from her house. She unbuckled her seat belt. "Thanks for the ride."

He caught her hand, and awareness crept up her

arm as she met his eyes. "Do you have plans tonight?"

Trinity glanced at her condo and back to his face. She should lie and say yes. She should definitely *not* spend more time with him. But instead of lying, she shook her head. "Not really."

"Can I buy you dinner?"

"I'm not very hungry." She held up her box of Cheerios. "Plus, I have cereal."

He chuckled, shaking his head. "You can't seriously still believe I had anything to do with the attacks on your friends. I'm on Team Muse. I always have been."

"I don't know what to think, but you sound pretty obsessed with fighting with Titans, so…" She bit back a smile. "No sense getting attached to a guy with a death wish."

He raised a brow. "Does that mean I'm off the 'Loath Entirely' list?"

She laughed. Again. "How did *you* find out about my list?"

"Just a lucky guess." He looked across the street, then back to her face. "How about if I confess that, secretly, I have every intention of living through this."

"I do have a concert coming up for a theater grand opening."

He nodded slowly. The intensity in his gaze was like a caress. "Nothing's going to keep me from being there to cheer you on."

Emotion choked her throat. "I believe you." And somehow she meant it.

He brought his hand up to cup her cheek. "Good."

He searched her eyes as he leaned in closer. Gods, he smelled like ocean waves and the forest all at once. His breath warmed her skin as her lips parted, her pulse racing with anticipation. What was she doing?

Wake up. You're falling for pretty words.

She moved back, away from the comfort of his touch. "I can't…do this."

"Yeah. Sorry." He straightened, but instead of anger, or even a little passive aggressive moping, he glanced her way with a hint of a smile. "Any chance you changed your mind about dinner?"

Clearly, he wasn't bent out of shape and butt-hurt by her rejection. It made her wish she'd kissed him after all. Gods, she was losing her mind!

She chuckled and put her seat belt back on. "Dinner sounds great."

CHAPTER 6

MIKOLAS MARVELED AT the woman seated across the table from him. Yes, she was beautiful. Her dark hair and deep brown eyes coupled with her full lips made him ache to claim that unfulfilled kiss, but it was her cynical humor and the melody that flowed through her like a song that had him enraptured. He'd never met anyone like her.

When she walked, her steps were a dance to a symphony no one else could hear, and while she pondered something, she hummed secret tunes under her breath. Trinity was a symphony of layers that he longed to explore. But her pain, the wounds from entrusting her heart to an unworthy man, shadowed her eyes. He yearned to hold her, to heal her.

As they left the restaurant, his cell phone rang. And it wasn't "That's Amore" this time.

"Hey, Ted," he answered, not wanting to hide anything from Trinity.

"I'm back in with Kronos." Ted's voice was hushed and breathless, and then a car door slammed. "I have until tomorrow night to get identification made for Iapetus. He'll be under the alias Ian Elys."

Mikolas stopped. "Did you find out what they're planning?"

"Kevin wants me to get them into the theater opening." Ted sighed. "Without Zeus busting out of his disguise and saving the day, I don't see a way for us to win this."

Mikolas shook his head slowly. "Not on our own." He glanced over at Trinity. "I'm going to visit Rhea. If Kronos settles his score with Zeus, his wife will be the next name on his retribution list. She has a vested interest in helping us."

"Okay." Ted cleared his throat. "How's Trinity?"

Mikolas ground his teeth, unwilling to go down this path with him while Trinity stood a few feet away. "She's safe. I'm going to keep it that way. Let me know if they move up the timetable."

Mikolas slid his phone back into his pocket and caught up with Trinity. "It was Ted."

She nodded. "I guessed as much."

"You might want to let Nate know Ted's back on the inside with the Titans. He also said they want him to get them into the *Les Neuf Soeurs* opening."

"Shit." She frowned. "Zeus needs to clean up this mess. We can't let them wander into the opening. You saw what his brother did at the Observatory. The theater will be packed, and if Kronos slows time, everyone will be sitting ducks for that spear-wielding psycho."

Mikolas nodded. "That's why I think we're going to

have to face them before the theater opens." Before she could remind him that it was a fight they couldn't win, he added, "Want to come with me to talk to Mrs. Zervos?"

She stopped at the car. "Do you think she'll help us?"

"I think if we lose, the Titans will be coming for her next, so there's a good chance she'll get involved." He opened the passenger door. "I also think it's no coincidence that she chose to live in Crystal City, just like her son."

Trinity got into the car and looked up at him. "You think they've been planning for this. My generation of muses got the dreams about the theater in Crystal City to lure us here to reopen *Les Neuf Soeurs* because the timing was right?"

He leaned on the door. "The Guiders of Destiny play a long game. I think they saw the Order would eventually crack into Tartarus. This is the intersection of time they thought would give humanity the best chance of defeating them. We're all here to take part in it."

She nodded. "The question is, whose story is ending?"

TRINITY WRUNG HER hands, wondering for the millionth time why she agreed to go with Mikolas to meet with Mrs. Zervos. A few months ago, Mikolas and Ted had been the ones to discover the elderly woman's true identity was Rhea, the Mother of the Gods. Until he had put the pieces together, none of the muses had realized she was more than just one of the retired women in Lia's, the Muse of Comedy, geriatric poker group. Along the way, they had also discovered that Cooper's grandmother, Agnes, was the Muse of Hymns for her generation.

The fog in Trinity's mind was beginning to clear. What if Mikolas was right about everything? It couldn't be a coincidence that Rhea and her two best friends, the Guiders of Destiny, ended up living on the same floor in Blessed Mary's Village as Cooper's grandmother. What if everything happening in Crystal City right now really *was* part of a bigger divine plan?

Mikolas parked in a visitor spot at Blessed Mary's and turned off the car. "You're pretty quiet over there. Not even humming tonight."

"I was just thinking about what you said earlier about all of us being here at the same time." She lifted her gaze to meet his. "Maybe you're on to something."

He almost smiled. "We're going to have a tough time convincing the others."

She chuckled, reaching for the door handle. "Especially Reed."

The wind tugged at her hair, stinging her cheeks as they walked toward the high-rise. Fall in Crystal City wasn't much different than summer. The days were sunny and warm, but the nights carried a chill on the sea breeze, foreshadowing the winter rain that would be visiting soon. They had hoped to get the theater opened back in August, but between Erica's wedding, and Mason healing up from the last showdown with Kronos, construction had been delayed.

So instead in their mid-August goal, the grand opening would be the first Friday of November. It had seemed so far in the future, but it was coming up faster than she realized now.

Outside of Rhea's room, Mikolas turned her way. "Ready?"

"To meet the Mother of the Gods?" She chuckled, shaking her head. "No, but…"

The door opened, interrupting Trinity mid-sentence.

A tall, slender woman with a short stylish angular cut to her black hair complete with silver highlights. Definitely Lia's handiwork. Not only was Lia the Muse of Comedy, but she was a wizard with haircuts and colors.

The elderly woman looked up at Mikolas. "I've been expecting you. Come in."

She offered her hand to Trinity. "I'm Mrs. Zervos, and you are?"

"Trinity Porter. Nice to meet you." She shook Rhea's hand and followed Mikolas inside without any further explanation. There were two more women on either end of Rhea's sofa and the Mother of the Gods took a seat between them. Although all three appeared to be retirees complete with crow's feet and frown lines, there was an otherness to their eyes, something Trinity couldn't quite describe. The colors of their irises were too vivid, their movements too fluid, too powerful.

Their hostess focused on Mikolas. "Zack told us his father is back with one of his brothers. Is this true?"

Mikolas nodded. "I'm afraid so. He brought Iapetus with him. I was hoping I could use your shard again to banish them."

She glanced at her cohorts on either side, then turned her full attention to Trinity. "I've seen you on the YouTube. Lia told me about you. You're the Muse of Music."

Trinity nodded slowly. Outside of her circle of muse sisters, she'd never discussed being a muse. "Yes, ma'am."

Mrs. Zervos's silver brow quirked. "Ma'am? No." She shook her head, a feisty smile curving her lips.

For a moment, a vision of Mrs. Zervos in her true form, with long red hair and violet eyes, flashed in Trinity's head.

Trinity rubbed her forehead, frowning, and Mrs. Zervos chuckled. "I mingle in your world as a harmless old woman, but I am still Rhea, Daughter of Gaia and Mother to the Gods."

"She meant no offense." Mikolas took Trinity's hand, his fingers lacing with hers before she realized what was happening. His deep voice was even and commanding. "Your husband could attack us at any time. Will you lend me the shard?"

Rhea smiled. "This is your muse. You found her."

The woman sitting on Rhea's right leaned forward. Her voice had an inhuman clarity and vibration to it, like a chime. "Your gift from the gods has awakened, Mikolas Leandros. You are the final piece to this destiny. But facing Kronos again is not your fate."

Goose bumps rose on Trinity's arms, and she gripped his hand tighter. This wasn't a senior citizen; this was the voice of one of the Guiders of Destiny.

Mikolas straightened beside her. "What are you saying? There's no way to stop him this time?"

Rhea patted her friend's knee and looked at Mikolas. "That is not what she said, Mortal."

Gods, why did they all speak in riddles? Trinity cleared her throat. "So this isn't decided yet. We can beat Kronos and save the world. Is that what you're saying?"

The three women shared a knowing look, and Rhea met Trinity's eyes. "We have watched a millennia pass by waiting for the moment when Zeus and his father would meet once more. The time has come."

Mikolas sighed. "Two more people died the other night because Zeus didn't step up. I won't stand by and wait for Kronos to exact his rage on Trinity."

Rhea clasped her hands in her lap. "Forgive me for being vague. I forget that mortals struggle to recognize a divine plan as it comes to fruition before them."

Trinity glanced over at Mikolas, wondering if the condescending attitude was bugging him, too. His profile was chiseled, determined, and emotionless. If he was annoyed, he wasn't letting it show. She made a mental note to never play poker with this man.

Her gaze fell to their joined hands, and as if he could read her thoughts, his thumb stroked hers. The simple touch had her heart racing and her mind struggling to focus on the goddess before her, instead of her own conflicting emotions.

Rhea crossed her feet at the ankles. "My son has had generations of daughters, muses like you. Every generation a few find their Guardians—most do not— and through it all, he kept watch over the Order of the Titans. The Guiders of Destiny had foreseen that Kronos would be freed from Tartarus; the only variable was when."

She glanced at her friends and back to Mikolas. "My son asked us to wait in Crystal City. Over the years, we've met many of my beautiful granddaughters, muses like Agnes Hanover and your friend Lia."

"We're very fond of Lia," one of the Guiders of Destiny chimed in as she primped her freshly styled hair.

Lia had become a part of their weekly poker group without ever realizing she was tossing nickels into a pot with the Mother of the Gods, last generation's Muse of Hymns, and the Guiders of Destiny. Now none of it seemed like a coincidence.

"Anyway," Rhea continued, "my son sent your generation the dreams because he recognized the Order was approaching their goal. This was the time for the muses to combine their gifts and inspire humanity to new heights."

Trinity rubbed the back of her neck. "Forgive me for not seeing the perfection in this divine plan, but what's the point of inspiring mankind when we're about to wiped off the face of the Earth by Kronos and his brother?"

Mrs. Spanos tsked. "Must you be so shortsighted? Zeus needs to convince his father that humanity is a worthwhile creation. You and your sisters represent the purest examples of the magic of mortality—art. You will open your theater, and the inspiration that pours from the doors will be a tidal wave of breathtaking beauty to spill onto the dry earth."

Rhea took over again. "Kronos can't be killed, and he can no longer be caged either, so if your race has any hope of survival, Kronos must grow to love humanity as much as my son does. Open your theater, brighten the world of man, and hopefully your gift will inspire mercy in my husband."

Mikolas slid his hand free of Trinity's. She tried to remind herself of her not-so-savory taste in men. Getting attached to this one only proved how flawed he must be.

"While Zeus is handling Kronos, are we to stand by

and do nothing as Iapetus slaughters innocents?" Mikolas asked.

The Guiders of Destiny shared a silent look before Mrs. Spanos met his eyes. "You have all the tools you need to stop him."

A muscle in his cheek began to tick. "Can you be more specific?"

"You were given a powerful gift from Zeus." One of the Guiders of Destiny raised a brow. "Use it."

All three women rose from the couch at the same time. Rhea opened her hands. "We have told you all we can. Open your theater. It is humanity's greatest hope."

Trinity got up and turned for the door, but Mikolas wasn't following her. He stood before the goddess and bowed his head. "We appreciate your wisdom and guidance. We will venture to fulfill our destinies and ask that you bless our paths."

Rhea placed a hand on his shoulder, and light shone all over the room. Trinity shielded her eyes, unsure what exactly she was witnessing. Rhea lowered her hand, the light dissipating as quickly as it had blossomed.

Mikolas lifted his head. "Thank you for your blessing."

He turned, and without another word, guided Trinity out of the apartment. He was silent until they made it back into the elevator. Once the doors closed, he met her eyes, his voice as tender as a caress. "Are you all right?"

"Yeah." She fought the urge to take his hand and crossed her arms instead. "What was that back there?"

"Gods and goddesses thrive on our praise and worship." He must've read Trinity's body language loud and clear because he faced the elevator doors, the concern and care gone from his voice. "I figured getting her blessing couldn't hurt."

The doors opened, and Trinity stepped out. "That's what the light show was?"

"Maybe?" He finally glanced her way, biting back a smile. "I've never been blessed by a goddess before."

She nudged him with her shoulder. "Do I detect a tiny bit of smart-assery?"

He chuckled, his gaze catching hers for a second. "I've never met anyone like you before."

She waited for a caveat, or a joke, or…something, but it didn't come. She rolled her eyes to deflect his comment. "You obviously haven't hung out with many muses."

"True." He caught her hand as they walked toward his car. "But I wasn't kidding. We sat in a room with immortals, and it never rattled you. You're brave, bold, and…being near you…" His eyes searched hers, her pulse kicking into overdrive. "You make me wish we could start over."

Heat flushed her skin. "Maybe if we live through this…we could try."

His lips curved into a crooked smile that made her heart flip. "I'm going to hold you to that."

CHAPTER 7

MIKOLAS WOKE TO "That's Amore" blaring next to his head. He swiped for his phone without opening his eyes. Rolling over, he put the cell to his ear.

"Nona, it's—" He squinted at the clock. "It's five thirty in the morning here."

"Sorry, Miko, but it's important."

He was wide-awake now. "Is everything all right?"

"*Nai.* We're fine. It's *you* I worry for."

Mikolas heaved a sigh of relief and sat up. "Why?"

She lowered her voice as if someone else on the line might hear. "You told me Kronos was free and you found your muse, but you rushed me off the phone before I could ask about your gift. Are you safe? Do you heal like your Papou?"

"No." Mikolas ran a hand through his hair. "But I'm safe for now. You should stay home until we find a way to protect everyone, though."

"Pshhh." He could almost see her swiping her hand through the air. "You need us, Miko. Plus, the tickets are the nonrefundables." She paused. "Tell me about her."

There was the real reason for her early-morning

call. Mikolas chuckled. "She's beautiful, intelligent, and has recently decided not to hate me."

"Your father played her songs for me on the computer. I closed my eyes and heard the magic." She sighed before abruptly changing the subject. "I'm bringing baklava. Does she like almond or…?"

He didn't know. There were some many facets to Trinity that he wanted to discover, but even a basic thing like her favorite foods reminded him that he'd barely scratched the surface.

"I'll find out."

"Good boy." He could hear her smile right through the phone. "Be careful, Miko."

"I will, Nona."

"We asked much of you to join the Order, and you did everything you could to stop their drilling. You took all these risks to help others, but now you've found your muse. Don't be a hero, Miko. Stay safe, fall in love. You've done your work for the gods. The rest is in their hands."

He rubbed a hand down his face. "It's not so simple. Kronos brought Iapetus with him this time. They'll kill more people. I can't stand back and let that happen. Love will mean nothing if we lose this battle."

"Ah, Miko," she whispered. "Love is the *only* thing worth fighting for."

She ended the call with her flight information and one more reminder to find out what kind of baklava she should make for Trinity.

He set his phone aside and went into the bathroom. He turned on the light and frowned. There was a raised, red rash on his shoulder. It was shaped like…a hand.

Rhea's blessing.

He leaned in for a closer a look. His skin wasn't hot to the touch, but it definitely looked like a burn of some kind. What had she passed on to him?

Trinity pressed the sustain pedal on the piano, allowing the chords to linger and fade, gradually picking up a meditative beat that matched her heart. She'd awakened this morning with an odd emptiness she couldn't put her finger on. It usually meant there was a song aching to break free. The melody would flow from her fingers, but she needed her partner in crime to help with the lyrics. Although, today, she did manage to scrawl a few poetic lines on her yellow notepad.

"Hey, Trin." Erica stood in the doorway with a Pop-Tart and two teas. "Hungry?"

Trinity slid her hands off the piano keys and reached over to grab her bowl of Cheerios. "I've got cereal."

Erica came over to the piano bench and nudged Trinity with her hip to scoot over. "You haven't called me with an urgent lyrics request in a while."

"You've got a husband and a baby now." Trinity scooched over and munched her cereal as Erica sat beside her. Trinity dropped her spoon back into the bowl. "I'm trying to respect the new boundaries."

Erica rolled her eyes. "I'm still your best friend." She set the foil Pop-Tart wrapper aside. "What do you have so far?"

Trinity smiled and propped up her notepad on the music desk of the baby grand. "It's not much yet, but I think this is the chorus." She ran through a few chords and softly sang the few lyrics on her notes.

"Regrets are all I have left,
"My heart's an empty hole.
"But now you're here,
"And I want to let go.
"Don't make me hate you,
"Don't hurt me more.
"Don't lie to me,
"I've been in love before."

She opened her eyes and looked over at Erica. "So?"

Erica pressed her lips together for a second, then snatched the pad and pen. "Is this a love song or a heartbreak ballad?"

"I'm not sure yet." Trinity closed her eyes, her fingers instinctively finding the keys. The melody poured out of her until she became one with the music.

When Trinity came back to herself, Erica had jotted a few more lines on the pad. She set the pen on the piano, her eyes shining with emotion. "Mikolas has you all mixed up."

Trinity frowned. "What?"

"This song." She pointed to the pad. "I can't write the words for this one."

"What? Why not?" Trinity picked up the pad, reading Erica's notation: *No one blames you for loving Ted. He was broken, not you.*

Tears blurred Trinity's vision. She blinked them back and looked over at Erica. "I can't do this without you."

"Yes, you can." Erica squeezed her knee. "This is the song of your soul. This is you, Trin. Get it out. It's going to be beautiful."

Trinity wiped her nose. "He scares the shit out of me. Last time I let myself fall…"

Erica shook her head. "That was last time." She searched her eyes. "Remember how I thought I was making men obsessed and nuts because of the muse inside of me? You told me I deserved a good guy. You told me I deserved Reed."

Trinity nodded, glancing at the notepad so she could keep her emotions in check.

Erica bumped Trinity's shoulder. "Well, I'm returning the favor now. Trust your gut with this guy, Trin. You're the smartest person I know."

"Fine." Trinity glanced at her best friend. "I'll write

the song myself."

Erica chuckled. "You know I was talking about your Guardian, right?"

Trinity bit back a smile. "I'll let you know how it turns out."

"You do that." Erica got up. "You're coming over to Mel's for the Halloween party, right?"

Trinity blinked, struggling to mentally plot out her calendar. Melanie's little girl, Maggie, was crazy excited for Halloween. Mel and Nate had started planning the party a few weeks ago, back when they all thought the nightmare with Kronos was behind them. "I didn't realize it was still on."

Erica nodded. "Nate told me at the meeting yesterday that if the world is ending, he's sure as hell not going to miss out on a single smile from Maggie and little Noah."

Nate had grown into the sweetest dad Trinity had ever seen. The man was a dangerous shot with a Glock and a take-no-shit detective, but at home, he hung up his holsters and his family was the center of his universe.

"I guess I can understand that." Trinity's eyes widened. "Gods, it's tomorrow, isn't it?"

"Yep." Erica munched on her Pop-Tart, leaning on the doorframe. "I got Hope an adorable little lion suit, and I'm trying to get Reed to be Gomez to my Morticia."

"I might come as a frustrated songwriter who just

lost her lyricist."

Erica rolled her eyes. "You're going to be fine."

The truth was, there were no guarantees this song would ever be finished if Kronos had his way. But Trinity clung to the normalcy of laughing with her best friend. "I guess I better find a costume."

"See you soon." Erica started to go, but she turned back. "You should bring Mikolas."

Trinity raised a brow. "I won't tell Reed you said that."

"It's not like they have to hang out, but all the Guardians will be there. Mikolas should be, too."

"You sure you're not just playing matchmaker?"

Erica shrugged, while doing a damned fine job of looking innocent considering she had the Muse of Erotic Poetry in her soul. "All I'm saying is, he's part of the team now, marked by Zeus to help us." Her gaze locked on Trinity. "And I believe him. He stopped Kronos once, and he never would have done that if he truly believed in the Order of the Titans."

"Fine." Trinity sighed. "I'll invite him."

"Good. See you tomorrow, Trin!"

Erica left, and Trinity returned to the piano, to her song. She tapped her pen against the paper. If only she knew how it would end.

TED FLIPPED THE new driver's license over and over as

he sat behind his desk. He couldn't escape the surreal emotions churning in his gut. Two immortal Titans were about to walk through his door, Titans he once thought would save this world, not end it.

He reached for his cell and clicked on the photo gallery, then on a file labeled *T*. The screen filled with an image of Trinity grinning, her arms draped around his neck after he'd finished his first vocal recital. It had been lifetimes ago. How different would his life have been if he'd never told his father the muses were coming to Crystal City, California?

Fuck. Wandering down that path led to madness. He couldn't go back in time, couldn't change the destiny laid out before him.

But he could still mourn the life he could have had. He'd never measured up in his father's eyes, but Trinity had seen more to him than he ever had. Her inspiration could have changed everything if he had been strong enough to believe in himself.

"Do you have the identification?"

Ted straightened in his chair at the sound of Kevin's voice. "Yeah, it's here."

Kevin adjusted his tie and approached the desk. He plucked the driver's license from Ted's hand and examined the photo. "This will do."

Ted peered past him. "Where's your brother?"

"On the beach. We're meeting him there. Come."

"I have plans." Ted frowned. "I did what you asked. I'm finished."

"Surely you're not...defying me?" Kevin arched a silver brow.

"No." Ted stood up. "I can rearrange my schedule."

He followed Kevin out of his office, down the elevator, and then left the Belkin Oil building and crossed into the parking garage in silence. Ted had nothing to say. Whatever Iapetus was doing on the beach, it couldn't be good. Dread dug its claws into his shoulders.

Kevin looked over at Ted. "You drive."

Ted didn't argue. The sooner this was over, the sooner he could get home, lock his doors, and pretend he was safe from the Father of the Gods.

Out of habit, Ted pulled out his keys and checked his cell phone as he approached his car. Nothing. Not that he expected it. Mikolas had arrived at the office early and had left without a word. Ted struggled not to allow himself to imagine Mikolas rushing out to see Trinity. Imagining them together was going to make him more insane than the what-if path he'd wandered down earlier. He ground his teeth and popped the locks on the key fob.

Both he and Kevin got in the car, and Ted started the engine. He turned to his passenger. "Which beach are we visiting?"

Kevin slid his designer sunglasses on. "Crystal Pier."

When they reached the beach, Ted had no trouble finding parking. Tourist season was long over by late

October. The beaches were uncluttered, giving the locals plenty of room to jog, bike, and skateboard. A few surfers rode the waves off the shore, and a couple of kids played volleyball, oblivious to the fact that the God of Time was among them.

Ted scanned the area for Iapetus. "I don't see your brother."

"Ah, you will." Kevin nudged him and pointed toward the water.

Ted squinted as a surfer hopped up on his board, riding the crest of a big wave. A smaller surfer came up to the right of the first—a woman. She glided across the curl and dove off the board as the wave crashed down.

Suddenly, the first surfer abandoned his board and vanished under the waves. He came back up with the woman under his arm as he swam for shore. He was shouting something.

Goose bumps rose on Ted's arms, and as they got closer, he recognized them.

Hunter Armstrong, the retired Navy SEAL, had his girlfriend, the Muse of Epic Poetry in his arms. He carried her out of the ocean as a second man grabbed his board and followed. Reed McIntosh. It had to be. The firefighter and Hunter had been surfing buddies for years.

Ted's head snapped toward Kevin. "Where's Iapetus?"

The Titan pointed at the waves. His brother

stepped out of the surf, his spear in hand and his eyes glowing a bright red.

Ted's pulse thundered in his ears. He had to do something. But what? "Someone will call the police. He can't murder someone on a public beach."

"She's not dead. Not yet anyway."

What did that mean? Ted tried again. "They're probably already calling 9-1-1 about a guy on the beach with a giant spear."

"Mortals cannot see the God of Mortality's spear."

Shit. That meant Reed and Hunter couldn't see it, either, and neither of them had been at the Observatory gala so they'd never laid eyes on Iapetus. They wouldn't recognize him.

"Wait." Ted looked over at Kevin. "But I can see the spear."

"Because I have lifted the veil from your eyes."

Iapetus approached them in a black wet suit. His eyes were a more human color now. "The Guardian called Hunter could hear my thoughts. It is the only explanation for him snatching his muse from the water before I could finish her. I did not discover the other Guardian's gift. His muse isn't here."

Ted's mouth went dry. "Why are you attacking them? I thought you were going to the theater opening to draw Zeus out?"

Kevin placed a hand on Ted's shoulder. "During my last visit, I discovered my son granted each mortal man a gift to protect his muse. We won't be walking into that theater blind. We'll know their strengths and weaknesses."

"But you can just stop time like you did after the dance recital."

Kevin nodded and finally spared Ted a glance. "One of them can move faster than time. And one of them was able to touch an enchanted crystal that should have killed a mortal." He turned to his brother. "This time, we will be ready for whatever my son and my wife put in our path."

CHAPTER 8

Mikolas left the office early, eager to check on Trinity. With Kronos and Iapetus on the loose, he couldn't shake the feeling that he should be with her. But she'd insisted she was safe with Mason and Clio, and he didn't know her well enough yet to press it. He'd placated himself by remembering that Mason was also a Lycan shifter. No one was going to be able to sneak up on him, and his wolf wasn't controlled by whether or not his muse was in danger.

For now, Mikolas was counting on Ted to alert him of the Titans plans. Tonight, Kevin and his brother were meeting Ted at Belkin Oil to pick up the fake ID for Iapetus, and Mikolas had no intention of being there. The Guiders of Destiny had been very clear: facing Kronos was not part of Mikolas's fate this time.

He parked outside the theater and got out. Mason was up on a ladder stringing lights over the courtyard outside. Mikolas approached, shielding his eyes from the setting sun. "Hi, Mason. Trinity said she'd be here today."

"Hey, Mikolas." He wiped the sweat off his brow. "Yeah, she's workin' inside on the sound system with the tech."

Mikolas started for the door and stopped. He went to the base of the ladder. "Can I talk to you about the Titans?"

Mason slid his drill into his tool belt and climbed down the ladder. "What's up?"

Mikolas crossed his arms, keeping an eye on the door to the theater. "I realize everyone has good reason to doubt my motives, but my priority right now is Trinity, and I don't think Callie's plan to ignore the Titans is going to work."

Mason rested his hand on the drill handle at his belt. "Why are you telling *me* this?"

"Because I've been giving this some thought, and all of our gifts from the gods are to protect our muses, so the powers don't kick in unless she's in danger, right?"

Mason nodded. "What's that got to do with me?"

"You're a Lycan. You can shift into a wolf and it has nothing to do with your muse being in peril. I'm also betting that since your family line was cursed by Zeus, when you're a wolf, you're immune to Kronos's magic. His ability to manipulate time wouldn't work on you."

"Damn." Mason chuckled, shaking his head. "You've been giving this *plenty* of thought." He rubbed at his chest, his Southern drawl forced Mikolas to focus. Although Mikolas was very comfortable with English, the southern accent made the words more foreign. "Even as a wolf, I'm not immune to bullets. Whatever you're planning, we'd need the others to make it work, and even then, we couldn't face two of those bastards. I understand where you're comin' from, I do, but this is Zeus's fight."

"And where the fuck is he?" Mikolas gestured to the empty parking lot. "He told me at the gala that he would handle his father, but that leaves us with Iapetus. He's the God of Mortality. He feeds on our deaths."

Mason's shoulders tensed, a glint of aggression lighting his eyes in contrast to his easygoing nature. "Look, I'm not happy about any of this, but I'm not shifting and rushing into a fight I can't win, either. There's too much at stake."

"But what if we *could* win?" Mikolas searched Mason's face. He didn't see a trace of weakness. Good. Mikolas tipped his head toward the door. "Help me get Clio and Trinity on board. I think if we can separate the Titans and work together as a team, we could stop Iapetus."

THE NEW SOUND system for the theater was installed, tested, and tweaked, and now Trinity treated herself to a little escape from reality. The tech left, and she put on her headphones, gripping the earpieces on either side of her head. With her eyes closed, the symphony of sound embraced her, swamping her senses in the glorious melody of Mozart's "Queen of the Night" aria. The high notes pinged with perfect clarity, dancing across her soul, alert and awake.

Suddenly she sensed she was no longer alone. She spun around in the sound booth chair to find Mikolas leaning on the doorframe, his forearm up by his head and a hint of a smile on his lips.

She'd been thinking about him earlier in the day while Clio had been peppering her with questions. Being the Muse of History, after Clio discovered the prophecy of the Guardians, she'd switched focus to researching each of the muses and their original partners in mythology. She had thought it might help them find their Guardians. It had worked for a few of them, but Trinity was another story. Euterpe's mate was Strymon, a mighty river god and king. Mikolas was from Greece, but he didn't have anything to do with a river and he was far from a king.

She crooked her finger, beckoning him over, and took off the headphones so she could turn one and press it to her ear, and put the other one to his ear. They hadn't known each other long enough for her to know what type of music he enjoyed, but he didn't seem to have an aversion to Mozart. The shared headphones kept him close enough that she could feel the heat coming off his skin.

He turned a little toward her. "Didn't take you for an opera fan."

She chuckled. "Muse of Music here. It's tough for

me to find a genre I don't like. Do you like opera?"

"Yes." He closed his eyes, listening. "My nona raised me on classical music."

The aria ended, and Trinity lowered the headphones slowly, her gaze wandering over his face. He had a strong chiseled jaw, a gentle mouth, and dark eyes she could lose herself in. She swallowed the lump in her throat. "I was going to finish putting on outlet covers backstage."

"Can I help you?"

She nodded without putting any distance between them. "That'd be great." Gods, he smelled good. "But before we go get to work, can I ask you something?"

"Yes." His voice had dropped to a throaty whisper that had heat coiling low in her belly.

For a second, she couldn't remember what she was going to ask, then blurted out. "Halloween."

He chuckled. "Not what I was expecting."

She grinned and straightened up, regretting the space between them instantly. "Sorry. In all the Titan craziness, I forgot all about it, but Maggie, Mel and Nate's daughter, is ten, and this is a major holiday in her world. In spite of Kronos breaking free, they don't want to cancel the party, and Erica said I should invite you since everyone else will be there."

He stared at her for a moment, and then stood up. "I wouldn't want to intrude."

She frowned and followed him to the door to the sound booth. "Wait, what?" She caught his arm.

He turned around, his eyes locked on hers. "Tell Erica I said thanks for the invite."

Trinity raised a brow. "*I'm* the one who asked you." Her hand found a place on her hip. "Aren't you the one who has been pushing me to trust you?"

"Yeah." He broke eye contact, examining the new ceiling. "Obviously I've been pushing too hard."

Trinity frowned. "What am I missing here?"

He ran his hand back through his hair, the wavy curls refusing to be tamed. "Is it that hard to understand? If you're asking me to go because you'd like me there, you might get a better response, but if you're only doing this because your friend pressured you, then…I've got plenty of other things I can do instead."

Trinity sighed and pulled him back into the booth. She sat down and pointed to the other chair. "Can we talk?"

He took the seat, but apparently, he was going to let her do the talking.

All right.

Trinity cleared her throat. "It was kind of shitty that I made it sound like I was only inviting you because Erica wanted me to."

He nodded slowly, but the corner of his mouth twitched—a crack in his butt-hurt armor.

Trinity shrugged. "I don't mean to constantly push you away, but in my defense, until very recently, I thought you gave the order to try to kill me."

He uncrossed his arms, resting his forearms on his

thighs as he leaned forward. "And part of me, the part that still mourns Nia, feels like I deserve it." He shook his head, his gaze falling to the floor. "Can I be honest with you?"

"I'm a fan of honesty." She gripped the sides of the chair.

He lifted his head, his brown eyes melting her where she sat. "My grandmother called me this morning and something she said has been bothering me." He focused on his hands. "She told me that love is the only thing worth fighting for." A sad chuckle escaped him as he met her gaze again. "But I've spent my whole life devoted to a sense of duty my grandfather planted in me when he explained I'd been marked by the gods."

He focused on his shoes. "I'm trying to tell you that I've never been in love. I don't know a damn thing about it. But when I think about Ted being the lucky son of a bitch who earned yours, I want to beat the living shit out of him for hurting you. The entitled prick had no idea what a gift he'd been given."

Tears stung Trinity's eyes as she reached out to cup his face in her hands. She waited for him to look at her, and she searched his eyes—for what she wasn't sure. Slowly, she leaned in closer and closer until her mouth was on his.

His lips were tender but strong, and they tasted sweet with a hint of salt—delicious. Every caress made her ache for more. His hands slid up her legs and around her back, rolling her and her chair closer to him. She tilted her head as his tongue parted her lips, exploring her mouth. Her fingers tangled in the back of his hair as their kiss grew more urgent. He held her tighter until she abandoned her chair for his lap, straddling him. His hands slid farther up her back, his fingers wide and possessive, singeing her skin with a desire she'd never known before. She ground her hips against him, enjoying the growl in his throat as his erection pulsed in his jeans.

"Oh!"

Trinity was off his lap and a couple of steps away in a heartbeat as she spun around to find Clio in the doorway. "Hey, Clio. Um. What's up?"

Other than Mikolas. Thank the gods she'd managed to keep that in her inside voice. Clio wasn't a virginal saint, but she was still the youngest of their muse sisters and the flush of color in her cheeks made it clear she hadn't meant to interrupt them.

"I…uh…" She glanced at Mikolas. "Hi." Her gaze snapped back to Trinity. "Mason left one of the drills on the stage with the rest of the electrical socket covers. He just wanted to be sure you knew it was there." She shifted her weight with a sheepish grin. "I better go see if he needs any help with the outside lights. Sorry about my timing." She cringed. "I should've knocked."

And then she was gone.

Trinity slowly turned toward Mikolas. He smiled up at her from under his thick black lashes. "How about I buy a lock for that door?"

She laughed. "Good plan." She released a pent-up breath, rubbing her hands down her pants. "For a guy who claims to have never been in love…that kiss was… Yeah."

"I was inspired." He chuckled, his smile taking on a sexy tilt that had her pulse racing. "And I said I've never been *in love* before." He stood up and took her hand. "Never claimed to be virginal."

"Point taken." Trinity pulled him out of the sound booth and headed down toward the main theater. She looked back at him. "Thanks for what you said back there. Maybe I really don't know much about love, either."

He lifted her hand to his lips and brushed a kiss to her knuckles. "Is that invitation to the Halloween party still open?"

"Yes." She jogged up the steps to the stage and picked up the drill. "I hope you'll come. And it has nothing to do with Erica."

He climbed the stairs and took her free hand. "I'll be there."

And something about the way he said it implied so much more than the party.

CHAPTER 9

TED TOOK OUT his phone to call Mikolas and warn him, but before he could press call, Kevin leaned down to the driver's side. Ted dismissed the screen and lowered the window. "Did you forget something?"

Kevin smiled, but his eyes were cold and calculating. "Keep your phone close. When we've discovered all of their gifts, I'll be in touch to plan our attack."

Ted swallowed the lump in his throat and tried to nod confidently. "You know my number."

"Yes. I do." He started to straighten up and hesitated, turning his attention back on Ted. "Remember where your loyalty lies, Mortal."

And just like that, they were gone. Ted checked the clock on his phone. Not even a minute had passed, but their car was no longer in the lot. Kronos must've slowed time, and now Ted had no idea which way they went, let alone where. The time manipulations were unsettling. It felt like he was losing his mind.

He took a deep breath and stared at Mikolas's name on his phone. Where did his loyalty lie? If he looked the other way, the Titans had promised his safety, but could he live with Trinity's and Mikolas's blood on his hands?

He pressed the button. His choice was made.

Trinity handed Mikolas another screw. He twisted it in the socket cover before finishing it off with the drill. It was monotonous work, but it gave him time to process that kiss. He hadn't been expecting it, but the second her lips touched his, a primal passion had ignited with an intensity he'd never known. He'd kissed plenty of beautiful women in his life, but this was…all-consuming. Gods, he couldn't shake the desire she kindled inside him.

And the instinct to protect her took on a new layer. This was beyond a duty; it was a need. He glanced up at her as he took the next cover and screw from her hand. "I think I came up with a plan to stop Iapetus."

She frowned. "It's not our fight."

"I think you're wrong." His phone buzzed, and he stood up to answer. "Ted? What's up?"

"They're trying to figure out each of the Guardian's powers. Iapetus went after Callie on the beach."

"Fuck." Mikolas glanced over at Trinity. "Is she okay?"

"I don't know. Hunter carried her out of the water, but Kevin said she wasn't dead yet. I don't know what that means."

"Thanks for the information."

"I'll be in touch. Watch your back." The phone went dead.

Mikolas stuffed it back in his pocket and lifted his gaze as Trinity's cell phone buzzed. She stared at the screen, the color draining from her face. "Mel says Callie's been injured. She's unconscious. We need to get to the hospital. Now."

"Ted just told me the Titans are testing us trying to discover each of the Guardian's abilities."

Trinity pushed her hair back from her face. "Then why hurt Callie?"

"Unless our muse is in danger we don't have any special powers." He took her hand. "We may not have time to wait for Zeus to fight this battle."

"Please don't press this." She looked up, and the pain in her eyes broke him. "I can't lose anyone else."

MIKOLAS KEPT HIS back against the far wall while Trinity, Erica, and Lia surrounded Callie's bed in the emergency room. The nurse kept trying to catch his eye, but he didn't glance her way. No doubt they had too many people in the small hospital room, but there was no way he was leaving Trinity.

Cooper strode down the hall in his paramedic garb, his jaw set as he entered. "What happened? Our rig didn't get the call."

Lia caught his arm, bringing him closer. "Hunter's

still talking to the doctor. Her foot was sliced open. They bandaged it, but she won't wake up."

He frowned. "Did she lose a lot of blood?"

"Not really, no."

Mikolas frowned. If Ted was right and this wound came from the Titans, any wound from Iapteus's spear was a mortal wound.

He moved closer to Trinity and whispered in her ear. "I think I know what happened." He looked at Cooper and raised his voice to a normal volume again. "You can heal her. I'll explain everything, but we need to close the wound first."

Cooper shook his head as he carefully inspected the wound on the bottom of her foot. "It doesn't work like that. Only if Lia's in danger."

"You saved Reed after the fire, right?"

Cooper nodded. "Sort of. Apollo did. He just did it through me. The force of his power nearly killed me."

Mikolas glanced at Trinity and back to Cooper. "I think I can keep you safe from it."

Cooper raised a brow. "Is this the demigod thing?"

"If I understood Zack correctly, yes. I don't have the full grasp of how it all works yet, but this isn't a shark bite on her foot. If we don't close the wound, she'll die."

Cooper frowned. "How could you possibly know that? It's not infected."

"This is a cut from the spear of the God of Mortality." Mikolas sighed. "We need to heal her and get her out of here."

Cooper took Lia's hand, his attention shifting to her. "I have to try."

Lia nodded, but worry lined her eyes. "Please be careful."

Cooper pulled in a couple of deep breaths as he cupped Callie's injured foot in his hands. Mikolas gripped Cooper's shoulder and closed his eyes. For a second, nothing happened. His heart sank. At the Observatory, he'd touched Cooper and the Guardian had been able to wake the others from Kronos's thrall. It should've worked with Callie's wound, too.

Suddenly, blinding light erupted in his mind. Mikolas struggled to stay upright. Heat seared his organs, and although his eyes were closed, somehow he could see Apollo inspecting him.

The God of the Sun came closer. "Who are you?" he asked in Greek.

"I'm the Guardian of the Muse of Music," Mikolas answered.

"How is this possible?" the god whispered.

"Zeus." Suddenly a bolt of pure energy shot through Cooper, and like a lightning rod it flowed right into Mikolas. The power overflow burned until darkness claimed him.

When Mikolas opened his eyes, Trinity was looking down at him. Her cool fingers stroked his hair. "Welcome back."

He frowned, peering around her. "I'm on the

ground."

"Yeah. Your legs gave out."

Cooper knelt beside her, holding Mikolas's wrist and checking his pulse. "Trinity made sure you didn't hit your head. Your pulse is strong. How do you feel?"

Good question. Mikolas rubbed his forehead. "Apollo. I saw him."

Cooper released his wrist. "Yeah, I don't know how you did it, but you took the brunt of the power surge."

"Is Callie…"

"She's awake," Cooper said. "Can you stand? We need to get you up before they stick you in a room here, too."

"I think so." His joints ached as Trinity and Cooper each took an arm and lifted him to his feet.

"Thank you, Mikolas." Callie's voice was faint, her face pale, but her exhausted smile warmed her features. "Whatever you did, it helped Cooper close the cut."

Hunter was on the other side of the bed now, holding her hand. His gaze shifted to Mikolas. A muscle clenched in his jaw, and a dangerous fury lit his eyes. "I heard that bastard's thoughts today. Callie dove in, and he was waiting for her down there under the waves. He was going to pierce her heart with his spear." He ground his teeth, probably censoring the rest of what he'd heard.

Mikolas nodded, fighting against the mental fog. "Ted told me that Kronos and his brother are working on discovering all the gifts Zeus bestowed on the

Guardians. Kronos is preparing for a showdown at the theater opening, and he doesn't plan on losing this time."

Callie shook her head. "We have to cancel the opening."

Trinity shook her head adamantly. "We can't. Let the gods fight. We're going to inspire."

Callie's skin was ashen, her eyes dull. She was a shell of the woman Mikolas had seen taking charge at the head of the table during their meeting. She wet her lips, her voice hoarse and tired. "Come on, Trin. They're going to kill everyone, and we can't stop them."

"You need to rest." Trinity took Callie's other hand. "The Muse of Epic Poetry inside you is going to kick your ass if she figures out you're trying to give up right now."

Mikolas focused on Hunter. "Iapetus must know you heard his thoughts since you pulled her up before she reached him. His spear barely wounded her foot."

Hunter kissed Callie's hand and met Mikolas's gaze. "But you said the cut almost killed her…"

"Iapetus is the God of Mortality. Our deaths feed him, and his spear is his conduit. He doesn't have to pierce someone's heart or decapitate them like he did at the gala in order to kill someone. One cut and he can slowly drain the life from a mortal, feeding on them slowly."

"Damn." Cooper ran a hand down his face.

Mikolas nodded, placing his hand at the small of Trinity's back. He needed to touch her, to know she was safe. "Callie will recover, but we have to stop him before the next muse isn't so lucky."

Cooper cleared his throat. "Mason and Clio are in the waiting room with Erica. Reed went to Callie's place to get them dry clothes."

Trinity glanced around the room. "What about Nate and Melanie?"

"Mel has a Halloween event at the high school tonight," Lia replied. "We called Nate, and he's bringing the kids over here. We'll watch them while he keeps an eye on Mel."

Mikolas nodded slowly. "I already talked to Mason, but I have an idea about how we might stop Iapetus."

Trinity caught Mikolas's hand before he could share his plan. "Can I talk to you outside?"

"Sure." He followed her out into the busy ER hallway. "What's wrong?"

"It would be faster to tell you what's right." A crease marred her brow. "Did you seriously talk to Mason behind my back?"

"It wasn't like that." He frowned. "You make it sound like I was hiding it from you on purpose."

"But you were hiding it just the same." She groaned, shaking her head. "We were together all afternoon and evening today, and it never crossed your mind to mention this new plan?"

"I tried." He shook his head. "You made it pretty

clear that you're against facing the Titans."

"You're right, I am," she agreed, only further confusing him.

He didn't discuss it with her, because she didn't want to talk about it. But now she was upset because he didn't talk to her? He crossed his arms. "I don't understand why you're upset about me talking to Mason. You didn't want to hear about it anyway."

Her jaw went slack for a second. "You seriously don't get it, do you?" She searched his eyes as she placed her hand over his heart. "The only way I'm ever going to get past this trust issue is if we're a team. That means no secrets."

He covered her hand with his. "Even when it's something that might upset you?"

She nodded. "It needs to be us against the world." She paused, and added, "I want us to be a team."

His pulse surged, and he lifted her hand to his lips. "I want that, too."

Her mouth hinted at a smile. "Then no more going behind my back to make plans to save the world."

He chuckled, rolling his eyes. "It sounds shitty when you say it like that."

"Well, that's how it felt when I found out about it in there."

The pain in her eyes gutted him. He shook his head. "I'm sorry, Trin. The last thing I want in the world is to hurt you, but this isn't a fight I can walk away from. The stakes are too high."

"That's why I think we need to be patient and wait for Zeus and Rhea's help."

"Mankind could be extinct before Zeus lifts a finger." He rested his forehead against hers, his voice falling to a whisper. "I'm not willing to allow some Titan asshole to destroy humanity before I get the chance to earn your trust."

She brought her hand up to caress his cheek. "If we weren't in the hallway of a busy emergency room, I would kiss you *so* hard right now."

He raised a brow. "Even though I want to kick a Titan's ass?"

"Well…" She chuckled. "Maybe you should tell me about your plan."

CHAPTER 10

"YOU TAKE GOOD care of her," Trinity whispered as she hugged Hunter good-bye in the hospital parking lot.

"Always." He stepped back and offered Mikolas his hand. "Thanks again, man, for helping Coop tonight. I owe you."

"Glad it helped. I'm still not sure how this gift of mine works." Mikolas shook his hand. "I hope Callie feels better soon."

Hunter nodded, then walked back to the car where Callie waited in the passenger seat.

She leaned over and called to Trinity. "Don't forget the Halloween party tomorrow night!"

"I won't." Trinity waved. "Rest up."

Hunter got in, and they drove away from the hospital. Trinity looked over at Mikolas. "Okay, so, where are we going to plot the end of a Titan?"

He shrugged. "My place?"

She smiled. "I've been sort of curious about where you live."

"I hope it lives up to your expectations." He took her hand, threading his fingers with hers. And instead of cautioning herself about his motives, she allowed herself to enjoy the growing connection between them.

She got into his black Mercedes, and a swell of the familiar uneasiness festered in her heart. "You said before that you didn't run over Cooper, but this car did, didn't it?"

He turned on the engine and glanced her way. "I went to bed that night and when I woke up, Nate and his partner were at my door asking about my car. I walked them right out to the garage. Would I have done that if I had known it was smashed up from a hit-and-run?"

All true. She buckled her seat belt, settling in. "Ted and his enforcer stole your car?"

"Yes." He drove out of the parking lot and headed for the highway. "Ted hoped to frame me so I would be arrested. Then he could take back the leadership of the Order. In his defense, it was Philyra's plan, and she wouldn't take no for an answer. I'm just glad no one was killed."

"Me too." She glanced out the window. "I'm sorry I keep busting your balls over all this. I'm still wrapping my brain around all the tragedy we've faced since we started restoring the theater and trying to figure out how to forgive myself. I don't want to make the same mistakes again. I can't."

The rest of the drive was quiet. She wasn't sure what she expected. What could Mikolas say?

He took the winding roads slowly around the cove.

The houses on the cliff overlooking the Pacific Ocean were decidedly out of her tax bracket. He turned into a driveway leading to a Spanish style home with a red-tile roof. It was at least two, maybe three times as large as her place. She couldn't wait to see the inside.

He clicked the garage door opener on his visor and waited for it to open. He pulled in and pressed the button again, his attention on the rearview mirror. When it was closed, he turned her way. "I wish there were something I could say to let you know you can trust me, but in my experience, trust has to be earned." His gaze wandered over her face. "So I won't make promises that I will be there when you need me, but I *will* be there, Trin. I'll show you."

Her heart fluttered at his declaration, not because it was what she wanted to hear but because she actually believed him. She brushed a tender kiss to his cheek. "Thank you."

She met his eyes, aching to taste his lips, but she opened her door instead, bathing them in the light from overhead. "We better get inside. You owe me a plan that will stop Titans, but also allow you to live to tell the tale."

"Zeus is handling Kronos. We only need to stop Iapetus. Easy." There was a spark in his eyes that made her knees weak.

She followed him into the house and gasped as she looked around. She'd imagined a billionaire oil businessman would live in a cold futuristic home. The beach house, which was really more of a spacious hacienda, had an open floor plan that any home renovation show staff would've killed for. From the door to the garage, she could see the entire kitchen, living room, and expansive wall of glass overlooking the Pacific. All the furnishings tied in the earth tones of the paint and whitewashed wood flooring.

It was a home, not a gallery.

She nudged him. "Not bad, I guess, if awe-inspiring living spaces are your thing."

He was quiet for a second, before his deep laughter echoed off the high ceilings. "It took me a second to understand."

"Sarcasm is probably tough to translate."

"Sometimes." He shrugged. "I started learning English in grade-school. By the time I finished university and got a job with my father's business, I spoke with American companies every day." His playful smile coupled with his messy dark hair made her toes curl in her shoes. "But no one has ever made me laugh like you do. You…make me happy."

He walked her into the sunken living room and offered her a seat on the sand-colored sofa facing the cove.

She sat down, staring out the dark window. "I bet it's stunning during the sunset."

He settled in beside her. "That's why I bought this place, actually. The realtor brought me here as the sun was dipping below the horizon, and I was sold." He glanced over his shoulder toward the kitchen. "Do you want a drink?"

"Nah, I'm fine." She met his eyes. "Just tell me what you told Mason."

MIKOLAS TOOK A deep breath. She wouldn't like his plan, but after the attack on Callie today, it seemed even more impossible to wait for the gods to settle their differences.

"As you know," he started, "Zeus told me he would handle his father, which leaves Iapetus to us. Mason explained how he killed Philyra by shifting into his wolf and how her magic didn't affect him. But then she threatened Clio, and his Herculean strength kicked in."

Trinity nodded slowly. "Yeah, he's massive as a wolf. Add in the superhuman strength and his jaws snapped her head right off her shoulders."

He nodded. "For now, Iapetus hasn't figured out Mason's power, or that he's a Lycan. If we can lure the Titan away from Kronos, we could lead him right to Mason's wolf."

Trinity straightened, shaking her head. "You're missing a really important piece of the puzzle. Just being a wolf won't be enough. He needs to be crazy strong when he attacks and that only happens if Clio's in danger."

"Or if I'm close enough to magnify his power."

Trinity raised a brow. "Okay…that could work." Her gaze locked on his. "But that means your demigod powers have to kick in, which makes me the bait."

"Maybe not, though," he said. "My gift worked with Cooper today and the only one in danger was Callie."

Trinity nodded slowly. "True…but I was with you."

He thought back to the gala. He'd been alone when he had tried to wake Ted from Kronos's magic and nothing had happened.

"Shit." His heart sank. "This isn't going to work. It's too risky."

She placed her hand on his thigh and gave it a squeeze. "So when it was just you and Mason in harm's way, this plan was a possibility, but if I'm nearby it's too risky?"

He covered her hand with his. "I'm not dangling you in front of the God of Mortality." Just thinking about it churned a pit of dread in his stomach.

She stared out the picture window into the darkness, her gaze distant. "But you could be on to something." He started to respond, but she glanced his way with a raised finger. "Just hear me out on this. What if I'm with a couple of my muse sisters and their Guardians. Then if Iapetus came after me, all of us would be in danger. That means *all* the Guardians powers would be activated at once."

It could work, but if it didn't, it would be catastrophic. But if they didn't stop the Titans, humanity was doomed anyway. His heart wrenched. It was an impossible choice. He shook his head, trying to refocus on the logistics. "Who are you thinking should be with you?"

"Clio, for sure, so Mason can be superstrong while he's a wolf. Hunter would be handy to hear the Piercer's thoughts before he makes his move, but I don't think we'll be able to get Callie on board for this plan."

"What about Nate, Gavin, and Cooper?" He had purposefully left Reed out of the equation. The firefighter would be more likely to attack Mikolas than the Titan.

Trinity gave it some thought, then met his eyes. "Nate needs to protect the little ones, but Gavin's superspeed could be a big advantage, and he's good with a gun. A bullet may not kill Iapetus, but it would probably slow him down. And we should keep Cooper close in case anyone gets injured. You could help him manage all the power if he has to call on Apollo."

"Maybe we can talk to them at the Halloween party tomorrow night."

She nodded and squeezed his leg again. "I bet Erica could get Reed on board, too."

He shook his head. "Not a good idea. I don't blame Reed for hating me, but we'll have our hands full as it is, and any distractions or fights among us could get everyone killed."

Her brow arched. "Do you even know what his gift is?"

"No."

"He can move things with his mind."

Ahh, now Mikolas could understand her eagerness to add Reed to the plan. But the firefighter had made himself crystal clear when he had told Mikolas how he felt about him. "We don't need it. Once Mason is a wolf with Herculean strength, I can help magnify his power even more. Iapetus won't stand a chance." He rolled his shoulders. "Reed has sacrificed enough. The guy died in that fire, and Apollo brought him back. I was the leader of the Order at the time. When he sees me, I'm a reminder of how close he came to losing everything."

"Maybe you're right." She pushed her hair back from her forehead. "I guess we can talk to everyone tomorrow night and see if we can get this plan off the ground."

He took her hand. "Thank you."

"For what?" She smiled.

"For listening. And for improving the plan. You've been part of this group much longer than I have, and I value your insights."

She squeezed his hand. "We make a good team."

Her words struck a chord in his chest. "I agree." He stood up and pulled her to her feet. "I think I owe you a tour."

She grinned, and the joy on her face took his breath away. Gods, he could get addicted to seeing this woman happy.

He walked her down the hallway, pointing out guest rooms and bathrooms. At the end of the hall, the ceiling vaulted up again in a tiled atrium that rose two stories. In the center was a grand piano, and in the corner, a staircase led up to his office and the master suite.

"No way." Trinity went straight to the walnut piano. She sat on the bench and opened the keyboard. "Oh gods. It really is." She turned around toward him. "This is an antique Euterpe piano. Do you know how rare these are?"

"It was my grandmother's. I took lessons on it for years, and she insisted I ship it to California when I moved here." He shrugged, staring at the EUTERPE in gold letters. "It never occurred to me that it was a sign until now."

"I've never seen one. Not in person." She looked over her shoulder at him. "Mind if I try it out?"

"I didn't know you played the piano. I thought the guitar was your instrucment."

She smiled and faced the keys again. Her fingers ran through a few scales faster than he'd ever heard, and certainly faster than he'd ever mastered. As she played, she answered. "I can play the piano, guitar, flute, and violin. Music is…me." Her eyes sparkled. "Sing me a song. I'll see if I can find chords."

"I don't sing." He chuckled. "I can barely play the piano."

She rolled her eyes. "I bet you can. You just need

the right inspiration."

He leaned against the wall, unable to wipe the grin from his face as she launched into the "Overture" from *Carmen*. She had it memorized. Impressive.

Her body rocked with the melody, and her hands danced over the keys, rising with the flourish of a concert pianist. She was a vision, pulling emotion out of every note, making his antique piano sing.

She hit the final chord and smiled at him. "What?"

"You're beautiful."

Color flushed her cheeks. "I thought it was the music."

"You *are* the music." Mikolas shook his head and came closer, standing in the crook of the piano. "This is going to sound stupid since we both know we're on the brink of extinction, but for what it's worth, I never dreamed I could feel this way."

She focused on the keyboard, coaxing out a soft, sustained chord. "What way?"

He struggled to find the words, but they wouldn't come. Instead, he leaned over and lifted her hand from the keys. "Come here for a second."

She got up from the bench and came around in front of the piano with him. He reached to close the cover on the keyboard before meeting her eyes. "I don't have the English words. I need to show you."

Her dark eyes sparkled. "I'm intrigued."

He drew her into his arms, pressing a kiss to the top of her head as he whispered, *"De exo niosi pote etsi os tora."*

She rested her head against his chest as they slowly started to sway, a slow dance to the music of their heartbeats. "What does it mean?"

He closed his eyes, drinking in the scent of her hair. "I have never felt this… This is new. These feelings."

There was no plan or an agenda, just a raw need to be near her, to touch her. As he embraced her, a melody resonated in his chest until he softly gave voice to the words. Gradually he recognized the tune, a Greek love song his grandfather used to sing to his muse when Mikolas was just a boy.

Trinity's breath teased his neck as she hummed along with him, harmonizing, making the song theirs even though she didn't understand the words. Maybe they didn't need them.

His heart pounded as he pressed his lips to her bare shoulder. She turned her head, her eyes meeting his. Her lips were so close to his, he couldn't resist the pull any longer. She returned the kiss, setting off a wave of passion he'd never known before. This wasn't a surprise like their first one had been, and it wasn't an urgent lust or surge of need. This kiss had him yearning to be closer, smoldering with desire to lose himself in her, like he'd finally found a missing part of his soul.

Her hand slid up into the back of his hair as his tongue tangled slowly with hers. She moaned into the kiss, and something ignited inside him. He needed to be closer. Now.

He bent his knees and scooped her up into his arms. She smiled, kissing him between each word. "If you drop me, I'll kick your ass."

"If we go down, we're going together." He laughed into her mouth as he ascended the staircase. "No way I'm dropping you."

He lowered her onto the king-size bed and laid over her, savoring the sweet taste of her lips. Gradually he broke the kiss and stared down at her, memorizing every curve of her face.

Trinity caressed his cheek. "I need to tell you something."

He turned his head, kissing her palm before meeting her eyes again. "Okay."

"We have horrible timing, what with the Titans wanting to wipe out the human race and all." Her smile couldn't mask the regret in her eyes. "But in case there is no tomorrow, I want you to know…I've never felt like this before either."

She searched his face, her index finger tracing his jawline. "I'm a different person than I was back in college—smarter, wiser, more jaded. But when I'm with you, you accept me just the way I am. I don't have to try to hide the wounded parts of myself. This is a gift I never knew I wanted or would ever have."

He kissed her forehead, his voice rumbling in his chest. "I've spent my life chasing a predetermined destiny, the son of a powerful man, none of it my choice, but I did what was expected. It was a charmed, empty life." His gaze locked on hers. "Until I met you, my life had purpose, but no meaning. You have given me hope, Trinity. Something to live for."

She ran her hands up his back. "Thank you for not giving up on me."

He chuckled and gave a lopsided smile. "You probably haven't noticed, but I'm very stubborn when there's something I really want."

She laughed, shaking her head, but gradually, her laughter faded as she looked up into his eyes. Her grip on his shoulders tightened. "I want you, too."

Hearing her say the words loosened the tenuous hold on his desire. He fused his lips to hers and surrendered.

CHAPTER 11

GODS, THIS MAN could kiss. She couldn't get enough of him. Grabbing fistfuls of his shirt, she tugged it over his head, only breaking the kiss long enough to toss it away. The heat from his skin soaked right through her clothes, enticing her to lose all barriers between them.

His hands slid up her sides, right underneath her top, pushing it higher. The second his bare abdomen pressed against hers, desire raced through her veins, her body aching to rush the tempo of the moment. She parted her legs, allowing his hips to sink even closer. His erection throbbed against her until she was cursing their clothes.

He covered her neck with hot, slow, searing kisses as he lifted her top over her head and dropped it to the floor. He stared down at her for a moment, and the passion smoldering in his eyes made her heart race. She ran her hand up his muscular chest, allowing her gaze to wander, but a red mark on his shoulder caught her eye. It looked like a burn.

She carefully touched the mark. "What happened? Is this where Rhea touched you?"

"Yes." He nodded, a sexy smile curving the corner of his mouth. "But the last thing I want right now is to talk about gods and goddesses." He popped the front clasp of her bra open and dipped his head. "You're all I care about."

He took her nipple into the heat of his mouth, and her breath caught. Her fingers tangled in the back of his hair, and he cupped her other breast, teasing the nipple until it tightened into a taut peak. She arched her back, offering herself to him.

His hands moved lower, unbuttoning her jeans. He lifted his head. "I have protection in the bathroom. Want me to go get it?"

She'd forgotten about everything except her need for him, but he hadn't. His voice echoed through her memory: *You're all I care about.*

He was proving they weren't just words. He *meant* them. It was her protection above his pleasure.

"Yes." She caught his arm before he got up. "And lose those pants on your way back."

He raised a brow with a sexy grin. "Will yours be gone, too?"

"I could arrange that."

"If only my gift from the gods was superspeed." He got up from the bed. "I'll be right back."

She ogled his backside until he disappeared into the bathroom. Then she shimmied out of her jeans and underwear. If someone had told her a couple of weeks ago that she'd be naked in Mikolas's bed, she would've busted a gut laughing. But so much had changed since then.

She got up and turned down the bed, sliding between the soft sheets. Propping her head on her elbow, she lay on her side facing the bathroom. Right on cue, Mikolas opened the door and returned to the bed with a foil packet—and nothing else.

Every inch of his tan body was chiseled and strong. When her gaze reached his face, he chuckled. "I thought we had a deal."

"We did." She threw the covers back, flashing him. "I'm a woman of my word."

His gaze caressed her skin as he set the condom on the night stand and slid into bed with her. He rolled her onto her back, his lips picking up where he left off, his tongue swirling around her nipple. His searing kisses trailed lower making her writhe with need. When he reached her naval, he peered up at her from under his dark lashes and pushed her legs further apart.

"Tóso ómorfi agápi mou," he whispered. "You are so damn beautiful, Trin."

He dropped his head down, feeding on her core, his lips and tongue driving her wild until she cried out his name. He hummed his approval against her, his tongue teasing her faster, more urgently. She grasped one of the pillows and tossed it off the bed so she could grip the headboard, rocking her hips into him as raw desire consumed her.

"Don't stop," she gasped.

He slipped two fingers inside her and coaxed her to the brink. "I want to taste you," he growled. "Come for me."

Hearing the hunger in his voice pushed her over the edge. Her orgasm rocked through her like a tidal wave, every muscle contracting. She couldn't breathe, but what a way to go...

He worked his fingers inside her slowly through the aftershocks and then kissed his way back up her body. He nibbled at her shoulder, and the tip of his erection brushed her opening, making her ache to feel him inside her, filling her. He reached for the condom, but she took it from him before he could tear it open.

"My turn." She rolled him over, kissing along his collarbone before she sat up over him.

She tore the foil packet and straddled his thighs. The desire in his eyes had heat pooling low in her belly. Already, her body yearned for his attention again. She swirled her index finger around the tip of his shaft, enjoying the way his hands tightened on her legs, his hips bucking toward her as she slid the condom down his shaft.

Leaning over him, she stared into his eyes, her hips hovering just out of reach. She kissed him, savoring the taste of his mouth, and then whispered, "I want you."

He gripped her hips, fusing his lips to hers as he guided her onto his erection, entering her completely. She explored his chest with her fingertips, her pulse thundering in her ears as her tongue wrestled urgently with his. She couldn't get close enough to him.

Mikolas held her tight and rolled them over, his thrusts slow and deep. She looked up at him, memorizing every angle of his face, the intensity in his eyes.

He rested his forehead on hers. "I never want this to end, but you feel too good."

"So do you," she breathed against his lips.

He kissed her again and slipped his hand between their bodies. His fingers rubbed her core in time with his thrusts. She moaned into the kiss, dragging her fingernails down his back and over the curve of his ass. She squeezed, encouraging him to go faster as she neared the edge again.

His hips slammed into her once more and exploded inside her. He kept teasing her, his fingers working faster until she was clenching around him, her orgasm engulfing her senses.

Breaking the kiss, he struggled to catch his breath. "That was…"

Trinity nodded. "Yeah…"

He rested his head on her chest while she threaded her fingers through his hair. Not only was her pulse racing like crazy, but her heart was curiously melty at the same time. After Ted's betrayal, she'd sworn off men completely, so she hadn't sex in a few years but she didn't remember any of it being as intense as this.

Mikolas finally lifted his head. "I'll be right back."

She nodded, and he slid free of her body. He disappeared into the bathroom again and returned without the condom. He got into bed with her, and she snuggled against his chest, her head resting over his heart. She closed her eyes, drinking in the rhythm of his heartbeat. His pulse was primal music to her muse, a song she recognized.

His hand caressed her back as he kissed the top of her head. "Can you stay here tonight?"

She came up with a million reasons she shouldn't—no clean clothes, no toiletries, no makeup. They were all valid excuses, but even so, none of them motivated her to get out of his bed, to leave the safety of his arms.

"I'd like that." She lifted her head. "But I don't have my toothbrush or anything, so I'll be scary in the morning."

He chuckled. "Takes more than that to scare me."

"Good thing." She settled back against his chest, her breathing slowing to match his, and gradually, she succumbed to sleep.

MIKOLAS WOKE UP with the sun and found Trinity curled up with all the sheets and blankets, like a beautiful muse gyro. He smiled and went to the closet. After pulling on a pair of sweatpants and a tank, he ventured downstairs for his travel bag. He ran his fingers through his hair a couple of times as he opened the coat closet. He frequently traveled for work, so he always kept his bag stocked with travel-size toiletries and toothbrushes. He grabbed a few things for Trinity and set them on the kitchen counter.

Since Trinity hadn't come down yet, he figured he'd make some breakfast. While he preheated the oven, he took out a glass dish of tiropita and a few eggs. He wasn't sure what kind of food she liked, but he hoped if he cooked a couple of different options, she'd find something she would enjoy. The Cheerios popped in his head.

He went to the cupboard. No Cheerios, but he took out the box of Cap'n Crunch and set it on the counter.

"I didn't take you for a fan of the Captain."

He turned around to find Trinity in one of his button-down shirts and nothing else. Suddenly, he didn't care about breakfast. His appetite wasn't for food anymore.

"I don't eat much cereal, but I do enjoy this one." He shook the box playfully. "Other than Cheerios, I don't know what kind of food you like."

She came into the kitchen and gave the glass dish of tiropita a long look. "What is this?"

"It's a Greek cheese pie. Sort of like…" He searched for a food she might recognize. "Quiche? But it has a flakier crust. Like a pastry."

She smiled up at him. "Sounds delicious."

He put the glass dish in the oven. "I guess we have a few minutes to get dressed while it warms up." He went to the counter and handed her the toothbrush and toiletries. "You might need to use my hairbrush, but I think the rest is here."

"Thank you." She took them from him and headed down the hallway, calling over her shoulder. "We better get it together fast. We need costumes for the Halloween party tonight."

He stopped in his tracks. "Costumes?"

She peered back at him with a mischievous grin. "Yep. And getting a costume on Halloween means we'll be stuck with whatever they have left."

He raised a brow. "That sounds…bad?"

"Not as bad as our costumes are going to be!" She laughed and jogged up the stairs.

He followed her, drinking in the sound of her laugher. Being with Trinity reinforced his determination to find a way to beat the Titans. He wanted more days of listening to her laughter and nights of worshipping her body. And he sure as hell wasn't going to let Iapetus be the reason he didn't get them.

CHAPTER 12

TED OPENED THE door and dropped a few treats in each teenager's bag. Not many little kids trick-or-treated in his area anymore. It was probably easier and safer for their parents to walk them through the stores in the malls or go to one of those Trunk-or-Treat events.

When his cell phone rang, he quickly closed the door. Kevin's name lit the screen, and Ted contemplated rejecting the call. But pissing off the Father of the Gods wouldn't improve his chances of surviving this hostile takeover of the world, so…

"Yeah?" he answered.

"I have a task for you, Ted."

Ted shook his head. "I already did what you asked."

"And you're not finished," Kevin said sharply. "Not if you want to live."

Ted raked a hand through his hair. "What do you need?"

"The Muse of Tragic Poetry is having a party tonight. You will take her from her house."

"Kidnap her? Why?" This was nuts. The Guardians would kill him. "The Order already knows that her

Guardian can touch things and get visions. You don't need to test the theory. What's the point in taking her?"

Ted's ears popped, and his head throbbed. He would've collapsed to the floor...if he could move. He tried to at least lower his cell phone, but his limbs didn't respond. It was as if he'd been encased in wet cement.

Shit.

The Titans appeared in his living room, strolling in as if they'd been invited over for a drink. Kevin gripped Ted's neck, squeezing until stars lit around the edges of his vision. "When I tell you to do something, you don't question me. Next time, my brother will feed on *your* worthless mortality. Are we clear?"

He released Ted, as well as time itself. Ted stumbled forward, choking and coughing, struggling for air.

Kevin went to the door. "We will meet you at Crystal Peak, where the Order used to gather. Be there by midnight with the Muse of Tragic Poetry."

Ted swallowed hard. "What if I can't get her?"

Kevin narrowed his eyes and shrugged. "You die."

TRINITY ADJUSTED HER purple Esmerelda hair ribbon and glanced at Mikolas. She bit the inside of her cheek to keep from laughing. Party City had been picked over by the time they showed up, so they had to take whatever was left in their sizes. Trinity ended up in a Disney costume from *The Hunchback of Notre Dame*, and Mikolas was sporting a Trojan soldier getup complete with toga and gold plastic Trojan helmet.

"I still can't believe I let you talk me into wearing this." He shook his head, staring down at his wardrobe. "You realize the Greeks fought the Trojans, right? This is the uniform of my ancestors' ancient enemies."

She looked up at him with a sheepish grin. "At least you make it look good."

He chuckled and took her hand. "No pictures tonight. My family would never let me live this down."

Trinity knocked on the door, and a pint-sized Ghostbuster with strawberry-blond ringlets poking out around her goggles opened it. Her eyes widened as she grinned and launched herself at Trinity. "Aunt Trin, you look amazing!"

Trinity hugged her and stepped aside to show off her soldier. "Maggie, this is Mikolas."

"You're her Guardian." Maggie offered her small hand in a very grown-up fashion. "We waited a long time for you to find her."

He took her hand in a solemn grip. "I came from the other side of the world searching for her."

"I'm glad." Dimples formed in her rosy cheeks as her smile brightened. "Come inside. We have Witches' Brew!"

Trinity caught his hand as they made their way past a few of Maggie's friends from school. They were all huddled around the television with game controllers. Callie was on the couch. She still seemed a little pale, but her Victorian costume was on point. Trinity came over and sat beside her. "So…who are you dressed up as?"

Callie looked toward the kitchen. "Wait 'til Hunter gets back in here with my punch. I think you'll get it then."

Trinity smiled and patted her knee. "How are you feeling?"

"Tired, but much better." She looked up at Mikolas. "That plastic sword makes the outfit."

He chuckled. "There are so many things wrong with this costume."

Hunter came back from the kitchen with two cups and not much else, but his loincloth made it clear who Callie was supposed to be.

"Tarzan and Jane?" Trinity raised a brow. "Can't believe you got Hunter to wear that."

"Please." Callie rolled her eyes and gave the biggest smile Trinity had seen from her since the attack. "He's got no shame."

Hunter handed Callie her punch and grinned. "No shame in being the King of the Jungle."

He balled his hands into fists, raising them to his chest, but Callie held up her finger. "No Tarzan yelling in the house."

"All right. I'll save it for later." Hunter winked. He sobered as he turned to Mikolas. "Any news from our inside man?"

Mikolas shook his head. "No, not since he told me that Kronos and his brother are trying to discover each of our gifts." Mikolas removed his cell phone from his Trojan belt and checked for any new messages. "I don't want to call him and alert the Titans we've been talking, but he'll contact me when there's anything new happening. For now, it seems they're still planning their attack for the theater opening."

The other muses and Guardians migrated to the living room, and Trinity watched Mikolas lay out the plan they'd worked out the night before. He was a born leader. For whatever charmed life he might've thought he had inherited, he was no entitled slacker. There was an inherent nobility in him, and it had nothing to do with his amazing costume.

Her phone buzzed in her pocket. She slipped it free and glanced at the message. Ted's name lit her screen with a short text.

I need to talk. Alone. Meet me in the courtyard.

This couldn't be good. She looked up at Mikolas, and his gaze landed on her as if he'd sensed something. Breaking eye contact, she focused on her phone trying to decide her next move. The last thing she wanted to do was fire up Hunter. Of all the Guardians, Hunter had the most reason to beat the living shit out of Ted, and he usually tried anytime her ex came around. But this time, Ted might have information.

She got up and pulled Mikolas aside. "Ted's out back. He wants to talk to me. I'll be right back."

"I'll go with you," he replied.

Trinity shook her head. "I can handle this. He's on our side, remember? You finish plotting with the others; I'll let you know what I find out from Ted."

His hand slid around her waist bringing her in close. He kissed her temple and whispered, "If you're not back in ten minutes, I'll be right behind you."

"Deal." She nodded and excused herself into the kitchen. Melanie and Nate still lived in his two-bedroom condo, and with the party in full swing, it was going to be tough to slip out unnoticed. Alone in the kitchen, she sent off a quick reply.

Working on it. What's going on?

His next text came through quickly.

Nothing good.

Another second passed before another text popped up.

I just want to talk. They didn't follow me here.

Trinity put her phone back in the pocket of her skirt and made her way for the door. Erica came out of the bathroom and came straight for her, blocking the exit. She'd been moments away from a clean getaway.

Her best friend was dressed up as a very curvy version of Morticia Addams complete with a cleavage-bearing, low-cut black dress. "Party's not over yet." Erica tipped her head toward the others. "Where are you going?"

"I just need to grab something from the car." Trinity sucked at lying.

Erica raised a brow. "Want some company? Reed's busy playing Mario Kart with the kids."

And not talking to Mikolas... That was the subtext.

Trinity hesitated and finally nodded. "Sure. But I'm not going to the car."

Erica chuckled. "I *knew* it. You're a horrible liar. What's going on?"

"Ted's in the courtyard. He wants to talk."

Erica's smile faded. "I still don't trust that guy."

"I know, but he's our inside man with the Titans. If he's got more news about their plans, then I want to hear it."

"Let me guess—" Erica lowered her voice "—he wants you to come alone."

Trinity shrugged. "It's not like I didn't tell anyone. Mikolas will come out if I'm not back in a few minutes."

"Well, I'm going with you."

Trinity glanced down at Erica's costume. "You're liable to make some new unwanted friends out there."

She rolled her eyes. "Oh please, look who's talking." She grinned, gesturing to Trinity's Esmerelda costume. "The corset has your assets front and center, girlfriend.

You look hot."

Trinity fanned out her full skirt. "Coming from the Muse of Erotic Poetry, I'll take that as a compliment."

Erica caught her hand. "So let's go meet that worm of an ex."

Trinity bumped her with her hip. "I'm supposed to be going alone, so you'll have to make yourself scarce."

"Fine." Erica rolled her eyes. "But I'll still be close enough to scream for help if he tries anything."

Ted glanced up from the bench as Trinity approached with her friend Erica right behind her. He shouldn't have been disappointed. He had no right, but that didn't change that he was. Trinity didn't trust him.

Erica stopped short, giving them a little privacy.

Trinity was dressed as Esmerelda from *The Hunchback of Notre Dame*, and he could almost hear her belting out "God Bless the Outcasts" in his head. She crossed her arms, her hip jutting out to the side in a defensive gesture.

Memories of the days when she used to approach him with a smile stung.

"What are you doing here?" she asked.

"I'm supposed to be kidnapping Mel."

Trinity's eyes widened, and she dropped her hands to her sides, balling them into fists.

He put his own hands up and took a step toward

her. "I'm not going to touch her. Or you. I just needed to…see you."

One last time.

Her rage faded as she frowned. "What's going on?"

"Kronos and his brother are waiting for me at the park up at Crystal Peak, but I'm going alone. I just came to warn you to be careful…and to tell you face-to-face how sorry I am. For everything…" His voice caught. He cleared his throat, forcing the words out. "Regrets are all I have left, Trin. The Fates gave me a chance to change my stars the day we crossed paths at school, but I blew it. You made me happier than I'd ever been, but I couldn't see myself the way you saw me."

She came closer, concern lining her brow. "Why are you telling me this?"

"Because when I get to Crystal Peak, my conscious will be clear. I want to know I made things right between us."

Trinity shook her head. "They'll kill you, Ted."

"It doesn't matter now." He tugged at the collar of his black T-shirt. His neck was bruised and red where Kevin had choked him earlier. "All this shit…this wasn't how any of it was supposed to happen." His voice pinched. "I thought I was saving the fucking world, Trin. I *believed* it. I convinced myself sacrifices were necessary for the greater good. But no good is coming. None of this has turned out like I thought it would."

The pain in her eyes only reinforced his self-loathing. The "sacrifices" were flesh and blood to Trinity. Her friends Nia and Polly were dead because of him.

He shook his head. "Mikolas has a plan to stop Iapetus. Tell him that tonight is his chance. I'll separate them. Just be sure he waits until Kronos leaves. He'll be coming for Melanie on his own so don't leave her unprotected. Hell, maybe Zeus will finally drop the old-man disguise and get involved."

She glanced at Erica and back to Ted. For the first time since college, there wasn't a trace of disgust in her eyes. "I'm going to get Mikolas. Maybe we can all go up there as backup."

"No. That's why I wanted to talk to you alone. He'll try to be a hero." A sad chuckle escaped his lips. "I tried so damned hard to hate that guy, but he's…he's a good man, Trinity. You deserve no less."

She shook her head. "Don't do this, Ted. There's got to be another way."

He looked up at the stars, steeling his emotions. "My whole life I've taken the easy way out." His gaze finally locked on hers. "Let me have *one* moment when I can be the man you saw when you used to look at me. If I can leave this world as that guy, I'll go out better than I ever dreamed I could."

Trinity stumbled forward and embraced him. He held her tight, closing his eyes and taking one last breath of her hair. He stepped back before he lost his nerve. "Tell Mikolas to be at Crystal Peak at midnight. I'll be sure Iapetus is alone." He swallowed the lump in his throat. "One more thing." She met his eyes. "I did love you, Trin. That part was never a lie."

He turned around and went to his car without waiting for a reply.

Redemption was all he had left.

MIKOLAS CAME OUT of the condo just as Trinity ran into Ted's arms. An unfamiliar shot of jealousy burned in his chest. What the hell was going on?

Before he could interrupt them, Ted was walking away toward the parking lot. Mikolas headed for the courtyard. Trinity and Erica were talking in hushed voices as he approached.

"What did Ted want?"

Trinity's face was pale. "We have to put our plan into action tonight. He'll be sure Iapetus is alone at the park at Crystal Peak at midnight."

"Where the Order used to meet?"

She shrugged. "I guess so."

Mikolas yanked off the helmet and pushed his hair back from his forehead. "We're not ready."

"We may not get another chance."

He stared into her eyes, part of him aching to ask her about what he'd seen, but there wasn't time. Instead, he pressed a kiss to her forehead and forced his emotions into a box. If they lived through tonight, he could ask questions later.

"We better tell the others." He started to turn, but she caught his hand. He stopped and faced her.

Her eyes shone in the dim light of the courtyard. "We have to make tonight count, okay?"

"We will."

Or we'll die trying.

CHAPTER 13

MIKOLAS FINISHED CHANGING his clothes and checked the time on his phone. They were meeting at the Crystal Peak parking area a mile from the Order's gathering spot at the base of the mountain. The Titans would be expecting Ted and Melanie, but seeing a line of cars would tip them off that the plan had changed.

All the children were with Hunter and Callie at their place since Ted had warned them Kronos would be coming for Melanie at the condo. The kids were oblivious to the brewing battle, and because Callie wasn't strong enough to face the Titans, Gavin and Tera stayed with them, too. If Kronos manipulated time, Gavin's superspeed meant he would still be able to move and protect the others. It was far from a perfect plan, but it was the best they could do for now.

The rest of them were headed to Crystal Peak, including Reed and Erica. Mikolas wasn't sure what to make of the firefighter, but he'd insisted on joining the effort. Maybe he saw this as his chance to stab Mikolas in the back, or maybe he finally realized that Mikolas was truly trying to help. Only the gods knew for sure.

But if Trinity and Erica trusted him, Mikolas would, too.

The Titans would be meeting Ted at the small amphitheater where the Order used to gather for rituals. Mikolas couldn't shake the guilt weighing on his shoulders as he led the group through the woods to the location. He'd never been a believer in the Order's mission to free the Titans, and he tried to stop the offshore drilling, but that didn't change the company he had kept when he'd arrived in Crystal City. It had made him suspect to this group, and it was tough to pretend he wasn't being judged—or that he didn't deserve it.

He stopped when they got to a small clearing. "We're about a quarter of a mile from the Order's meeting spot." He looked over at Mason and Clio. "How long does it take you to shift?"

Mason met Clio's eyes before answering. "Shifting into a wolf is fast and painless. It's gettin' back that's tricky."

Clio took his hand. "I'll help you find your way back."

"I know you will." He bent to kiss her forehead. "See you soon, darlin'."

Mason disappeared, deeper into the forest, and Mikolas turned to face the others. "If Kronos is still at Crystal Peak, he won't be able to freeze time on Mason. As long as Trinity is nearby, I think I can shield us from his magic, too, but I can't be certain."

Reed crossed his arms over his chest. "Just to be sure I understand... We're going to rile up a Titan to chase us into the woods where he can be ambushed by a Lycan wolf."

Trinity stepped forward with a nod. "And Clio will stay with Mason, so the second the Titan with the spear shows up, she'll be in danger, and Mason's Herculean strength will kick in. If luck is on our side, Iapetus's head will pop off as easily as Philyra's did."

Reed didn't look convinced. "That seems awfully easy."

"If you have a better idea, now's the time." Mikolas rubbed his shoulder over the mark from Rhea's blessing. It itched, burning like his birthmark did when Trinity was in danger. He didn't know what it meant, but he didn't have time to analyze it right now.

Reed shrugged. "I'm not a fan of putting Erica in harm's way just to fire up my powers."

"Then we finally agree on something." Mikolas ground his teeth. "I hate it, too, but Zeus stacked the deck. We either work together with our muses or go at this with no superpowers. Your choice."

Reed glanced in the direction Mason had gone. "I have an idea." His gaze shifted to Mikolas. "You're sure Kronos will be out of the picture?"

"When Ted shows up to the meeting empty handed, Kronos will go after Melanie and leave Iapetus to deal with Ted." Mikolas rolled his shoulder back, trying to shake the burning under his shirt.

Reed nodded. "That Titan with the spear will smell a trap if we all show up at once. Cooper and I should stay here with the muses while *you* lure him to *us*."

Trinity shook her head. "No way." She locked eye with Mikolas. "What if he catches you? We'll be too far away to help, and your gift isn't going to come alive without me there. I'm going with you."

"No. Reed's right." Mikolas took her hand. "Can we talk?"

She sighed but nodded, following him a few paces from the group. He kept his voice hushed. "Rhea gave me her blessing, remember? It's burning right now. I think my power might work without putting you in harm's way."

A crease lined her brow. "We have *no* idea what her blessing did to you. You're just guessing what power it has. It's is too risky, and you know it. Let's stick to the original plan."

He brushed his finger over the smooth skin at the top of her hand, staring into her dark eyes. "Trin, Reed's idea makes more sense. If we all go, Iapetus will be defensive. The fight will start before we can get him to Mason."

Worry shone in her eyes. "Don't do this, Mikolas. It isn't your destiny."

"It is. Because my nona was right." He squeezed her hand. "Love is the only thing worth fighting for."

Her eyes widened, and she searched his face. When she spoke, her voice was determined. "No. Don't you dare tell me you love me and then walk into a battle you can't win."

"I don't have to *win*. I just need to stay ahead of him when he chases me." Mikolas embraced her, pressing a kiss to the top of her head. "And I do love you, Trin."

"No." She shoved against his chest, stumbling back a couple of steps. "If you loved me, you wouldn't be changing the plan and facing the God of Mortality alone. Love is a partnership. You don't get to make life-and-death decisions without me."

"I have everything to live for, and I have the blessing of the Mother of the Gods." He shook his head. "This will work. I can feel it."

"You dare to come to me empty handed?" A furious roar blew through the trees, shaking the ground.

Kronos.

Mikolas tensed. Ted must've arrived. The clock was ticking. As soon as Kronos left, their plan would roll into action.

He turned back to Trinity. "This is the only way."

Without waiting for a reply, he spun around and raced toward the sound.

TRINITY STARTED TO follow him, but Erica caught her arm. Trinity's eyes narrowed on her best friend. "Let me go."

Erica shook her head. "What are you going to do, Trin? Not even a bullet is going to stop that Titan. You're going to get yourself killed, and then Mikolas will die trying to save you."

Hearing Erica say 'Mikolas will die' out loud broke the barrier around Trinity's heart. "What if his plan doesn't work?" Her voice hitched. "What if he dies?"

Reed came up beside Erica, but his attention was on Trinity. "I'm the first to admit that I hesitate to trust the guy, but I've seen the way he looks at you, the way he tries to protect you. He's already stopped Kronos once, and this time, he just needs to lure that thing back to us. He can do this, Trinity."

He narrowed her eyes at them. "What if he needs help?"

Sympathy lined Erica's eyes. "Come on, Trin. What are you going to do? We can't stop a Titan with music."

"No. But there's a flare gun in Cooper's first aid kit."

She broke free of Erica's grip, bumping Reed aside with her shoulder as she marched back toward the Cooper and Lia. None of them understood. After Ted's betrayal, she'd shut down her heart. While one by one, her muse sisters had fallen in love, she had compartmentalized her emotions. She'd been happy for every one of them; they deserved men worthy of their gifts, their hearts. But she did not. Not after Trinity had given her heart to a man who had hunted them, who had brought on two of their deaths.

Fear and regret had kept her from trusting another man, from making another mistake. But Mikolas had shattered her well-built defenses. His patience, his confidence, and his gentle strength had broken down her barriers. Never pressuring her, always giving her the power, his love had come with no strings or expectations, and it had started to restore her faith in herself, in her judgment. If she lost him now, she'd never recover. He'd awakened her from the emotional wasteland of numbness, and she didn't want to go back.

What if she had finally found the other half of her soul and the gods cut his life short before she got to tell him how much he'd changed her life, how much he meant to her? He had walked into her world with the quiet power of a summer storm, washing away all the hurt and betrayal, and giving her a fresh new start.

Trinity straightened, her jaw set in determination. If the gods thought they could steal that from her now, they had another think coming.

MIKOLAS STALKED THROUGH the darkness toward the amphitheater. The pain in Trinity's eyes haunted him with each step, but he'd make it up to her when this was over. There was no other way.

As he neared the clearing, he spotted Kronos and

Iapetus standing over a body. Mikolas squinted, trying to get a better look. It was a battered and bruised Ted. In that instant, Mikolas understood what he'd seen earlier tonight with Ted and Trinity. He had been saying good-bye. He had made his choice to defy the Titans he'd spent his life trying to free. And they would kill him for his disobedience.

Iapetus raised his spear above Ted's body, and Mikolas stared up at the stars, struggling to convince himself there was nothing to be done now. This was Ted's destiny, his redemption.

"Wait." Kronos grabbed his brother's arm. "This is too quick. He deserves a long, painful torment before we grant him the peace of death."

Mikolas glared at the immortals through the foliage.

Ted slowly lifted his head. His face was bloody and swollen, but there wasn't a trace of fear in his eyes. "The longer you toy with me, the more likely it is that Melanie and Guardians will see my text and escape. They could be anywhere by now; you'll never find them."

Iapetus reached for Ted's hand and stretched his fingers apart until the knuckles popped and the skin tore. Ted let out a shriek as the Titan tossed his pinkie finger into the dirt.

Fuck. An honorable death was one thing, but this? A slow torture? Mikolas couldn't hide in the darkness and witness it. This wasn't redemption. Even though this was going to fuck up the plan, he had to do something.

Ted sobbed, spittle flying from his lips as he struggled to stand. He clasped his injured hand and shouted, "Tear me apart, you inhuman assholes. Killing me will save the muses. Trinity will live. That's all I care about." He held up his bloody hand. "I've got nine more fingers. Let's do this."

Kevin straightened his suit jacket with a growl. "I'll go collect the muse. You finish this, Brother."

Iapetus nodded, all his attention on his prey while Kevin strode toward the parking lot. Ted had done it. He'd separated the Titan brothers. Mikolas hadn't realized Ted possessed so much courage or fight.

Then it hit him. Ted had fucked things up on a monumental scale, but this, this moment proved Nona's declaration once more. Love was the only thing worth fighting for. Ted truly had loved Trinity.

Iapetus grabbed Ted's hand, wrenching his arm up, and Mikolas bolted into the clearing. He rammed his shoulder into the Titan's back so hard that both Iapetus and Ted fell to the ground, Iapetus's spear dropping with them.

Mikolas picked up the legendary weapon and pointed it at its owner, pinning him to the ground. "Let him go."

Iapetus smirked, but there was a flicker of something else in his eyes. Not fear, but wonder, perhaps. "No mortal can grasp the Piercer's spear," he boomed.

Mikolas ignored him, instead speaking to Ted. "Run. Go!"

Ted scrambled to his feet, grasping his wounded hand. His disfigured mouth warped his speech. "Kronos is going to—"

"I know," Mikolas cut in. "Thank you. You've done enough here. Go!"

Ted nodded and turned toward the parking lot, lumbering forward with a broken gait.

Mikolas pressed the tip of the spear harder against Iapetus's chest. "Get up."

"I don't take orders from mortals."

A thin trail of blood trickled from the spot where the spearhead pierced Iapetus. *Maybe the spear can kill an immortal!*

No way to know unless he tried…

Mikolas leaned all his weight on the weapon, and the sharp point sank through the Titan's skin, lodging deep in his chest.

Iapetus just laughed, grasping the spear with both hands. He jerked it free of his chest, as well as Mikolas's grip. Blood ran down his abdomen as the cavity filled before Mikolas's eyes.

Fuck.

Mikolas scrambled, putting distance between he and the God of Mortality as Iapetus lifted his spear. But Iapetus didn't throw it. Instead, his jaw dropped, his lips forming a silent O. Ted was standing behind him, his chest heaving, and sticking out of the Titan's neck was the jeweled dagger Mikolas had once used to make a blood oath with Ted.

Behind the wounded immortal, Ted staggered backward, but he wasn't fast enough.

The Titan spun around and buried the spearhead in Ted's abdomen. Blood trickled from Ted's mouth as his wide eyes searched for Mikolas. "Save her. Protect Trinity." He gasped, his eyelids fluttering as he forced out one last breath. "Run!"

Ted's final command snapped Mikolas into action. He pivoted and sprinted toward the forest. Before he reached the woods, though, fiery pain seared through his thigh, slamming him to the ground. The impact with the hard earth knocked the air out of his lungs. He coughed and tried to inspect his leg, despite the agony. His heart sank. The Piercer's spear had gone all the way through his thigh. He'd never make it.

Trinity's voice echoed in his memory: *Don't you dare tell me you love me and then walk into a battle you can't win.*

No. Giving up wasn't an option.

He gripped the spear, screaming as he yanked it out and tossed it aside. Stars danced at the edge of his vision, but the second the weapon left his skin, the pain faded. His eyes widened as he checked the wound. It was gone.

But there was no time to think about that now. He scrambled to his feet and ran. Iapetus slowed, probably to retrieve his weapon.

Shit. Mikolas should've taken it with him.

But it wouldn't matter if he could just get Iapetus back to the others, Mikolas reminded himself. Mason's mammoth Lycan wolf would finish the Titan. Mikolas had to push through, had to pump his legs faster.

His stride widened, even though the dim moonlight barely cast light on the trail. Bushes rustled and branches snapped behind him. He didn't bother looking back; he knew Iapetus was coming. As he neared the others, Mikolas slowed. He hated leading the God of Mortality right to the woman he'd only begun to know, to love, but they needed their Guardian gifts to kick in. Whatever Zeus's reasoning had been for requiring the muses to be in danger of the gifts to surface, it meant that to have any chance at eliminating Iapetus from this world, they had to work together.

Wind whistled past Mikolas's ear, and pain lit across his shoulder, the spear grazing his skin before piercing a tree ahead of him. But he kept running. He was almost there. Each step became more labored, his shirt more and more drenched in blood. The Titan would have probably already caught him if he hadn't had to stop and retrieve his spear.

Why wasn't he healing?

Suddenly, Trinity stepped into the clearing, both arms raised to eye level, her hands gripping a flare gun. Mikolas stumbled past her, and she fired straight at Iapetus. The flare lodged in the Titan's chest, the red fire casting an eerie glow on his face.

Iapetus clutched the spear in one hand, and reached for the flare with the other. He roared as he wrenched it free and dropped it to the dry earth. As he turned to face them again, an impossibly large wolf burst from the underbrush, racing toward the Titan. Time seemed to slow as the Lycan launched into the air, his jaws open, lips curled back in a deadly snarl. But Iapetus raised his spear, slamming the tip right through the Wolf's chest. A pained yowl escaped the animal as the Titan flicked the spear, sending the wolf vaulting into the shadows. His body hit the ground with a hollow thump.

Clio screamed, but Erica held her back from running to the fallen wolf. Cooper and Lia rushed in to pull the muses back from the fight. Mikolas squinted. Where was Trinity?

"Fuck!" Reed rushed forward in front of Erica and Clio, and suddenly, boulders came free of the earth, flying at Iapetus.

Reed's gift. They still had a chance.

The Titan laughed, batting the massive rocks away with one hand while the other clenched the shaft of the spear, still gleaming with Mason's blood.

Mikolas fought the fatigue. He had to help Reed, but he could barely lift his head.

Trinity rushed in and knelt beside him. Thank the gods she was safe for now.

"We need to get you out of here."

Reed hit the Titan with another boulder. Iapetus

roared in fury, crushing the granite with his bare hands.

"I don't understand." Mikolas reached up, touching his wounded shoulder. "I healed before. His spear went through my leg, and I healed instantly."

Movement caught his eye. Clio, Cooper, and Lia skirted the fight to tend to the wolf. Mikolas groaned. The plan was crumbling as easily as the boulders in the hands of a Titan.

That was it. He needed to touch Reed with his hands, to magnify his power. But his shoulder was still bleeding out, his life with it from the cursed spear. He was too weak to stand.

Mikolas gripped Trinity's wrist. "Get me up. I've got to get to Reed."

Trinity looked at him, disapproval and fear swirling in her expression, but she hooked his uninjured arm over her shoulder anyway. She struggled to get him upright, but when she did, they stumbled toward Reed together. Mikolas ground his teeth to fight the exhaustion the spear's wound was bathing him in.

Reed glanced at them over his shoulder. "What the hell are you doing?"

"Giving you enough power to decapitate a Titan." Mikolas placed a heavy hand on Reed's shoulder. "Aim for his head."

CHAPTER 14

THE TIME HAD come. He'd waited a millennium for destiny to converge on this moment, this lifetime, and now the future of the entire world rested squarely on his shoulders. He'd learned much since the last time he'd faced his father. He'd tasted the humility of being forgotten, written into fiction like Homer's *Iliad* or transformed into a glowing cartoon on the big screen while the muses sang about Hercules.

But this time there would be no theatrics—no thunderbolts, no cyclops, no Olympians coming to his aid. The fate of the world would not be fought on a public stage. Not this time. But before the showdown, he had one last thing to do.

Zack knocked on the door.

Nate, the police detective and Guardian of the Muse of Tragic Poetry, opened the door with his gun drawn.

Zack lifted his hands and allowed his mortal disguise to fade. The glow of his Olympian skin reflected in the mortal's wide eyes.

Nate's jaw went slack. "You really are Zeus."

He nodded. "Yes. And my father will be here soon.

Go collect the children and the others. Take them to the theater. My mother is waiting for you there." Zeus clasped Nate's shoulder. "I'm sorry I couldn't help you and the others sooner. I've waited too many lifetimes for this moment; there is much at stake. I couldn't risk revealing myself too soon."

Nate holstered his weapon, the shock of meeting a god fading from his eyes. He cleared his throat. "Just tell me what to do to protect my family."

Zeus lowered his hand and kept his voice hushed. "There's no way to stop Kronos. Tartarus will no longer hold him, and unlike Philyra or Iapetus, my father can manipulate time itself. There is no sneak attack, no physical way to kill him. He is a force of nature."

Nate cursed under his breath. "You're not inspiring much hope."

"No." Zeus shook his head. "The last time the Olympians faced the Titans, the entire world was nearly destroyed. I plan to save it once more, but it won't be through killing or trapping my father."

The detective frowned. "You're talking in riddles again."

Melanie came up behind her husband, wonder on her face. "Okay, I knew you were Zeus but…you *really* are Zeus. The God of Thunder is on my welcome mat."

Zeus chuckled. "Go, children. If I'm successful, we can celebrate at the theater opening."

"And if you're not?" Nate asked, lifting a brow.

"There won't be any humans left to attend."

TRINITY'S LEGS TREMBLED as she supported Mikolas's weight, her heart pounding like a drum in her ears. He and Reed were trying to hit Iapetus with a boulder, hoping it might knock the Titan's head free of his shoulders, but all she could think about was dragging Mikolas over to Cooper and having him heal Mikolas next. But what if Mikolas was too weak now to handle the surge of Apollo's power?

Erica came around to the other side of Mikolas, wrapping her arm around his waist and bearing some of the weight. She looked over at Trinity, tears in her eyes. "I love you, Trin. If this is it, I'm glad we're together."

"This isn't the end." Trinity gritted her teeth. "This asshole is not going to keep us from opening our theater and kissing our future children. We are *not* dying today." She glared at the Titan, then took a slow breath, pulling air deep into her diaphragm. She braced her legs against the ground and let out a deafening, high-pitched note that carried all her fear, pain, and rage.

For a split second, Iapetus stopped his forward progress. Blood was dripping from his forehead, his skin having been torn open by the rocks Reed had been launching in his direction.

Mikolas grunted to Reed. "Get...Cooper's...scalpel." He coughed. "Take his...head off."

Reed glanced at the paramedic working on Mason, and his jaw clenched. Sweat soaked through Reed's shirt as he focused his power, and then Cooper's medic kit fell over and the contents dumped out onto the ground. Almost faster than Trinity could see it, the sharp blade shot through the air and sliced open Iapetus's neck. Blood spewed down the Titan's broad chest, but he didn't fall.

The sick monster just laughed. "You mortals merely delay your inevitable destruction."

He dropped his spear, and Trinity nudged Mikolas. "The spear." She looked from the Titan's weapon when Mikolas didn't respond. His eyes were closed and his head had lolled forward, but his hand was still clamped tightly on Reed's shoulder, determined until the end.

This was not going to be the end. No fucking way.

"Reed!" She raised her voice a notch. "The spear! Mortals can't touch it with our hands, but you don't have to hold it...Use it!"

Reed's entire body tensed visibly, and the legendary weapon rose from the dirt and turned on its master. The spearhead pierced the Titan's wounded neck, straight through. Iapetus gurgled, his head cocking back exposing his severed spinal cord as he collapsed to the ground.

Trinity's stomach roiled at the carnage, but it had worked. It was over.

Reed spun around, blood trickling from both his nostrils. "We...we did it."

His elated expression darkened, and Trinity followed his gaze to Mikolas. His hand that had been on Reed's shoulder through the battle now dangled at his side. Lifeless.

"Cooper! I need you!" Trinity shouted, praying to the gods that his healing power would still work, even with Iapetus gone. "Now!"

Reed quickly helped Erica lower Mikolas to the ground. Trinity's legs were rubbery as she stumbled over to where Cooper, Lia, and Clio worked on Mason. Mason was a man again, but the gaping hole in his abdomen was far from healed.

"Mikolas needs help." Watery tears welled up in Trinity's eyes, obstructing her vision.

"I'm losing Mason. I need to summon Apollo." He looked over at Reed and Erica with Mikolas. "Can they bring Mikolas over here?"

Trinity shook her head. "He's too weak. Iapetus did something to him. He needs you, too. He's..."

Cooper scooped up his bag. "Keep pressure on the wound," he instructed Clio and Lia. "I'll try to patch Mikolas up enough to help us save Mason."

Clio nodded, but the pain in her eyes made it clear she knew the love of her life was dying. Gods, Trinity couldn't face losing anyone else. She ran back to Mikolas and dropped to her knees beside him. She took his hand, holding it tight. "Hang on. Please."

He winced, and a weak moan escaped him.

Cooper pulled out his scissors and cut Mikolas's shirt up the middle to get to the wound in his shoulder. Trinity's eyes widened. The blade of the spear had sliced right through the handprint from Rhea's blessing. Could that have cursed the gift from the goddess?

"Is this from the Piercer's spear?" Cooper asked.

Trinity nodded, biting back tears. "Yes. It got him in the leg, too, but Mikolas said it healed. Why isn't this one healing?"

Cooper shook his head, meeting her eyes. "This is just like the wound on Callie's foot. His life is draining out."

"We have to stop it."

"Dammit," Cooper cursed under his breath. "No human medicine is going to do that."

Mikolas squeezed her hand, and Trinity leaned down close to him. His hand was cold. Too cold. "I'm here," she said softly.

He blinked, staring up at her. "We need Apollo. He's the only one who can heal the spear's cut."

"You're too weak." Trinity shook her head. "Summoning him knocked you out when you were healthy."

"No choice." He winced. "Help me touch Cooper."

Lia came over and knelt beside Trinity. Her eyed were red and swollen. "We have to try, Trin. It's our only hope to save them both."

Trinity shrugged off her comfort. "No. We'll find another way."

Mikolas whispered, "*Stin kardiá mou*...You are in my heart, my soul." He swallowed, wincing again. "We have to try. If I start to fade away, sing to me. Your spirit will call to mine."

Trinity shook her head. "You don't know if that will work. No. Please."

"We don't know it won't." He closed his eyes. "We have to try."

Cooper reached over and took Mikolas's other hand. "I'm ready when you are."

Trinity sobbed. "Please don't. I can't lose you."

"You won't. I'll find my way back." He clasped Cooper's hand but looked deep into her eyes. "Sing."

Trinity's pulse surged. How could she sing when her world was crumbling before her eyes?

Erica crouched beside her, swiping a tear from her cheek before she wrapped her arm around Trinity's shoulders. "Your song. Now. You can do this, Trin."

Her song. The song of her soul.

She closed her eyes, her voice cracking on the first few words as she began. But gradually, her tone strengthened as light flashed on the other side of her eyelids. Apollo's light. Cooper and Mikolas had summoned the God of the Sun. It was happening.

"Regrets are all I have left,
"My heart's an empty hole.
"But now you're here,
"And I want to let go.

"Don't make me hate you,
"Don't hurt me more.
"Don't lie to me,
"I've been in love before."

She hadn't written the second verse yet, but somehow the words and melody flowed from her heart directly to the universe, to the gods.

"You taught me to trust,
"Your patience was my gift,
"And if you leave me now,
"Nothing on Earth will fill that rift.
"But I can't hate you,
"And I won't ever hurt you,
"Because you've shown me,
"I've never been in love before.
"Until now, in your arms,
"I found my home.
"I found my love,
"When I found you."

As her voice faded out, she opened her eyes, terrified of what she might see.

Mikolas looked like hell, but he smiled up at her and whispered, "I'm not leaving you, Trin. You brought me home, too."

CHAPTER 15

Zeus rose from the sofa inside the darkened home of the Muse of Tragic Poetry, his ancient heart thundering in his chest as his ears gave a tiny pop.

An immortal had just left this plane.

Iapetus. It had to be.

The corners of his mouth twitched. The Guardians and their muses had done it, just as the Guiders of Destiny had foretold.

Eons ago, after his final battle with Kronos and the Titans, Zeus had gone to his mother and consulted with the Guiders. They had warned him of the day his father would return and the ensuing war. Their visions were always murky, shaped in the mists of mortal free will, but one of the possible outcomes had pointed to mortals felling a mighty Titan without any help from immortals.

That vision was why he had forged the prophecy for the muses. His daughters would be reborn into mortal women every generation, and he would mark mortal men to be their Guardians and bless them with a gift from the gods in order to protect his daughters.

If the moment came that the muses and their

Guardians faced a Titan alone, their combined gifts might level the playing field. At least that had been his hope.

And now it had come to pass.

Perhaps this world could be saved after all.

Zeus hadn't laid eyes on his father since he had banished Kronos to Tartarus at the center of the Earth so many millennia before. Much had happened since that day. The mighty immortals had faded into myth and legend; they were figures in literature now, not real beings with passions and desires or capable of envy and hate.

Suddenly, Zeus noticed the silence. Outside the condo, the night birds had ceased singing, dogs had stopped barking, no children were laughing.

Time had stopped.

The front door opened. His father had dropped his mortal disguise, standing before him in his true form. His windblown white hair and bronze skin accented his bright silver eyes. They flashed with power and rage.

"My brother has left this world," Kronos growled, his hands balled into fists.

Zeus allowed the glow of his Olympian skin to cast shadows on the walls around them. "He is stardust, once again."

"I will destroy this world and every mortal in it until my brother is avenged and you and my wretched wife are destroyed." His eyes glowed with immortal power.

The light emanating from Zeus intensified, brightening the space around them as electricity snapped in the air. "I don't want to fight you, Father."

Kronos let out a disgusted laugh. "No, you expect your children to fight for you. You are a coward."

"Caring about humanity doesn't make me a coward. This world is worth saving. You may never have noticed humanity, but the mortals revered you. You gave them the Golden Age of Man—milk and honey, no wars, no hunger. You and your brethren shepherded humanity into being."

Kronos crossed his arms over his chest. "They're vermin. They don't live long enough to bother caring about them." He shook his head. "Why are you so concerned about them?"

Zeus took a step closer. "Because they have something we will never understand," he said. "Hope."

"Hope is futile." He scoffed, shaking his head. "We're stronger, faster, more powerful, wiser…"

"And yet, they have children and love them unconditionally, knowing full well that they will be separated from them eventually. Their finite days on this plane become precious in a way we'll never fully comprehend." Zeus gestured to the photos of Maggie and Noah hanging on the wall. "They have hope that their children will change the world for the better." He focused on his father again. "They don't need eternity. Doesn't that intrigue you at all?"

"No," Kronos said flatly. "You and your mother conspired against me. I will have my revenge."

Zeus's skin surged brighter again. "To what end, Father? Your thirst for revenge is all you have left. What if there could be more?"

Kronos opened his arms. "I'll rebuild this world to suit me and the Children of Gaia."

Zeus raised a brow. "Without humanity to worship all of you?"

"Are you and your mother truly willing to sacrifice your lives to save the worthless human race?" He frowned, his brow furrowed. "I don't believe it."

"If I can convince you they are worthy, and that there is room for all of us here, would you give up this assault on this world?" Zeus crossed his arms, gauging his father's reaction.

"As if you could ever do that." Kronos took a step closer, pointing at Zeus's chest. "Bring me your mother, and we can discuss your banishment from this plane."

Zeus shook his head slowly. "Give me a chance to show you why I treasure humanity. There is no victory in a family war."

"No," Kronos bellowed. "No more chances. It's time for retribution." Immortal fire flashed in his eyes.

Zeus opened his hands, laying his bet on the table. "A game, then."

Kronos frowned. "A game?"

"Yes." Zeus kept his emotions buried, his expression neutral, praying his father would be unable to resist the temptation. With all the time in the world, immortals were drawn to games like moths to bright light. "I will meet you in the park with a Petteia board on Friday. If I win, you will give up your vendetta against mankind and accompany me to the opening of *Les Neuf Soeurs* in peace."

"And if *I* win?"

Zeus chuckled. "You won't."

Kronos raised a brow. "You are cocky, my foolish son."

"No, I am confident."

Kronos clenched his jaw, but he'd taken the bait. "If *I* win, you will bring your mother to me and face the punishment of my choosing."

"Done." His mother wouldn't be pleased to discover Zeus had bet her life on a game, but this was a bet he didn't have any intention of losing.

WITH TRINITY'S HELP, Mikolas made his way over to Clio and Mason. Through Cooper, Apollo had closed the cut from the spear, but the healing hadn't regenerated Mikolas's strength. Between the blood loss and the overload of heat and light from Apollo, his legs were rubber and his strength was nonexistent. He feared one more jolt from Apollo could kill him.

Cooper knelt beside Mason, putting his fingers to

the other man's neck. "His pulse is weak and irregular, but he's alive."

Mikolas ground his teeth, fighting the fatigue that hollowed him. He was an empty husk, in no condition to tap into a god's power, but he had to try. This plan had been his idea. Mason's blood would be on his hands.

Trinity helped him sit without falling. Her dark eyes met his, concern plain on her face. "I suppose I'm wasting my breath by telling you that you look like hell and this is a bad idea."

Somehow, on the edge of the abyss, Trinity coaxed a smile from him. She was magic, his muse. He took her hand, losing himself in her eyes. "I need to do this. And I have every intention of making all of this up to you…if you'll let me."

She rolled her eyes, blinking back tears. "You're the most stubborn man I've ever met."

He kissed the back of her hand. "Like a mule." He looked over at Cooper and gripped the paramedic's shoulder. "I'm ready."

Cooper took a deep breath and then placed his hands over the open wound in Mason's abdomen. "Come on, Apollo. One more time."

Mikolas closed his eyes, wincing as the searing otherworldly heat crept up his arm. As it reached his heart, his muscles seized. The pain was so intense, he *wished* he could die. But in the pit of agony, a balm came to him. A melody. A familiar tune.

His reality split into a surreal yin and yang. A power overload ravaged his muscles and organs on one side, but on the other, he was safe in Trinity's embrace. She hummed into his ear the Greek folk song he'd shared with her. Somehow, without understanding the words, Trinity had memorized it, and the simple tune filled his head with recollections of his family, of holding Trinity in his arms. The warm remembrance embraced his battered soul, protecting his exhausted spirit. She kept him grounded in this world through her music.

Suddenly, the heat vanished. Mikolas groaned with relief, but he couldn't speak, or even open his mouth. He rested against Trinity, oblivious to the rest of the world. She was his world, his lifeline.

Her lips brushed his, breathing her life into him. "Stay with me, Mikolas. Please."

He wanted to tell her he was still there, but forming words seemed impossible. The worry in her voice tugged at his weak heart. Every part of him ached, the darkness tempting him to surrender, to escape the pain and bone-weary fatigue. Cooper shouted something. He felt compressions. his rib cage cracking under the repeated pressure.

It would be so easy to fade away...

Finally, the assault on his beaten body ended, and a warm drop of something fell on his forehead, followed by one more. Trinity's voice whispered through his mind like a siren's song.

"I love you."

CHAPTER 16

Trinity cradled Mikolas's head on her lap. Tears fell from her eyes as she surveyed his pale, beaten body. Because he had taken the extra power from Apollo, Cooper and the God of the Sun had been able to heal Mason. But Mikolas's already weakened body had taken even more punishment from Apollo's jolts of raw energy.

Reed and Cooper had done all they could to help Mikolas, but without a hospital and a defibrillator, Cooper couldn't get Mikolas's pulse into a sinus rhythm. The compressions had cracked his ribs, and they couldn't be sure if they were keeping him alive or causing more damage.

She whispered the words straight from her heart, praying he could still hear. If he crossed over, she needed him to know that through all this tragedy and death, he'd been her shining light. The song she'd finished earlier had been a stark truth that she hadn't allowed herself to see until that moment.

In a short period of time, Mikolas had shown her real love, honest and strong, and it made her realize that what she'd thought she'd had with Ted had never been any of those things. Ted had used her. And as much as she wanted to save Mikolas, she couldn't bear to see him suffering.

She bent forward, her lips caressing his. "I love you." His skin was cool to the touch, but she could have sworn he kissed her back.

Wishful thinking.

She started to straighten up when his hand slid into the back of her hair, and he *most definitely* kissed her back. Applause broke out around them, and she opened her eyes to find Mikolas staring up at her. He was beat to hell, but damn, his smile was heaven.

"I love you, too," he whispered. "Is Mason…"

"I'm good," Mason answered. "Healed up already."

Cooper grabbed his medic bag and went into action, checking Mikolas's pulse and blood pressure, but Trinity kept the majority of her attention on Mikolas. He was alive. He had survived. They both had. Gratitude swelled in her chest.

Reed stood over Cooper. "How are his vitals?"

"Not great, but considering he almost died three times tonight…" Cooper shrugged. "He's still with us."

Reed glanced over his shoulder. "We need to take care of the body over there. I have no idea what a Titan's DNA might look like, but it's probably best that we make sure he doesn't end up in the medical examiner's office."

"And Ted." Mikolas grimaced, sucking in a pained breath as he looked up at Trinity. "He's gone. He saved me, so I could protect you."

Ted had told her his plan earlier tonight, and she had known they would kill him, but deep down, she hadn't believed he would go through with it. She frowned. "I...I didn't think he'd really..." She shook her head. She had plenty of reasons to hate him, but in the end, he'd given everything for a chance at redemption. The lump in her throat surprised her. "I warned him not to go."

Mikolas reached up to cup her face, his voice raw—far from his usual rich baritone. "He knew what he was doing. I told him to run, but he came back to help me anyway. He didn't live a hero's life, but he died as one."

Her eyes welled with tears. "Why are you telling me this?"

"Because without him, I wouldn't be here in your arms." His thumb stroked her cheek. "And you were right about him all along. Your judgment wasn't off, Trin. It just took him longer to see himself like you did."

His declaration rocked her to the core. Dammit, she wanted to hug him so hard right now, but she refrained, for his ribs' sake. At the same time, her loathing of Ted Belkin gradually morphed into pity, maybe even a little grief.

Trinity wiped her nose, struggling to process all the emotions brewing inside her. "He told me you were a good man." She kissed Mikolas's forehead. "Understatement of the year."

He took a slow breath and winced. "I might need help getting back to the car."

Reed and Cooper moved to either side of Mikolas. Reed looked at Trinity. "Let's get him up, and then Coop and I will deal with the Titan."

They lifted Mikolas to his feet and steadied him. Trinity stood in front of him. "Can you stay upright?"

"I think so," Mikolas replied.

Cooper didn't look convinced. "Maybe Lia can help you get him back to the car?" He glanced at his muse. "We'll be right behind you guys."

"What about Ted?" Trinity asked.

Reed looked over at Iapetus and back to Trinity. "If we bury the big guy and give Nate a heads-up about where he is, then we can call the police about finding Ted's body. Nate can be sure no one finds Iapetus, and unless the police has Kronos and Iapetus's fingerprints on file, Ted's murder will go unsolved."

Mason eyed the body. "I've got a shovel and a post-hole digger in my truck. I can help Trinity get Mikolas back to the parking lot, and I'll come back with some tools."

"Thanks, man," Reed answered.

Cooper opened his bag and took out a penlight. He turned to Reed. "While they're getting tools, I can check you over, too."

Reed frowned. "I'm fine."

Cooper raised a brow. "Your nose is still bleeding."

"I'll be all right," Reed said, dismissing it. "I've just

never used my gift with the power boost I got from Mikolas."

Erica put a hand on her hip. "Stop being a pain in the ass, McIntosh, and let Cooper do his job."

Reed chuckled and held out his arm for the blood pressure cuff. "Fine."

Lia and Erica stayed with the guys while Mason and Clio helped Trinity and Mikolas hobble back to the parking lot.

Trinity looked over at Mason. "How are *you* feeling?"

His southern accent softened the horror of the night. "I'm feelin' fine now, but that was closer to death than I ever care to come again. I was lookin' down at our bodies there for a bit."

Clio shook her head. "Let's never get that close to saying good-bye again, okay?"

He chuckled. "I'm good with that plan, darlin'."

Mikolas glanced over at Trinity. He didn't say anything out loud, but his expression warmed her all over. His eyes were making promises his body couldn't possibly deliver on right now.

Her phone buzzed, and fear seized her heart. In the terror of the evening, she'd about forgotten about Kronos going after Mel. Gods she was a horrible friend.

Callie's text lit up her screen.

Are you all right?

Trinity let out a sigh of relief. Thank the gods they

were safe. "Kronos must not have shown up at Mel and Nate's. Callie wants to know if we're all right."

She fired off a quick reply.

We're battered but still standing. Are you guys safe?

Waiting for a response seemed to take forever. Finally, her phone lit up again.

Come to the theater and we'll tell you everything. Short version: Zeus dropped his disguise tonight.

Trinity's eyes widened as she pushed her cell back into her pocket. "They're waiting for us at the theater. Apparently, Zeus is finally getting involved."

"About fucking time," Mikolas rasped. He started to laugh and then winced. "Ow."

They headed for the cars in silence until Mason broke it. "Why am I all healed up and you aren't?"

Mikolas shrugged. "I don't know how any of this works, but maybe since I was taking the overflow of Apollo's power, he didn't have time for Cooper to get everything fixed without killing me?"

"Makes sense." Mason nodded, helping him over an exposed tree root. "So he just fixed the mortal wound from the spear?"

"I guess?" Mikolas replied. "My ribs still hurt like hell."

Trinity cringed. "That's probably from Reed. Your heartbeat was abnormal, so he was doing chest compressions to make sure you were getting blood to your brain."

"He saved my life." A muscle tensed in his cheek. "I'll have to thank him later."

When the parking lot came into view, Trinity smiled. "I have never been so happy to see a black Mercedes."

Mikolas chuckled and then groaned. "You're just excited that you're going to get to drive it."

"That too." She grinned up at him, the reality of the night settling on to her shoulders. "We 'mere mortals' toppled a Titan."

"Team effort." Mikolas smiled. "The flare gun was a good idea."

Trinity opened her mouth to respond, but Mason stopped at the passenger side of Mikolas's car and cut in before she could get a word out. "I need to say somethin' before you go," he said. "I thought your plan was gonna work tonight, or I never would have agreed to it. I didn't think about the Titan's spear, either." He shook his head. "Just don't want you to think I'm castin' blame on anything but the Titan."

Mikolas took Mason's hand. "Thanks, Mason." He looked over at Clio. "Sorry tonight went to shit."

The Muse of History pushed her glasses farther up her nose with a studious smile. "Some of the best victories in history came about when well thought-out plans went to shit. We're in good company."

Trinity got Mikolas settled into the passenger seat and closed the door. She gave Clio and Mason a hug and jogged around to the driver's side. "See you guys at the theater."

Rhea frowned as Trinity and Mikolas limped into the theater. "What happened?"

Mikolas leaned against the wall. "We defeated Iapetus."

"But you're wounded." She glanced over her shoulder to her constant companions, the Guiders of Destiny, and back to Mikolas. "That's impossible. I gave you my blessing."

Trinity cleared her throat. "You also failed to mention what it was supposed to do."

Rhea raised a brow. "He should have been impervious to injury, like Achilles. My son made him a demigod, but the status is useless in a fragile mortal body."

"It wouldn't been nice if we had known that *before* we faced Iapetus." Trinity grumbled.

Mikolas cleared his throat, hoping to distract his muse. Insulting goddesses was never a great idea, even when you were right. "Gifts from the gods often have many catches."

Mikolas took Trinity's hand. Touching her made the aches and pains fade into the background. He shifted his gaze to Rhea. "Zeus granted us gifts, but they only work when our muse is in danger, so I'm only a demigod if Trinity is nearby, and your blessing apparently doesn't work on my shoulder."

"The spot where I touched you became your weak spot, like Achilles's heel." Her eyes widened. "How are you still alive? His spear slicing your shoulder should've delivered a mortal wound."

"We had a little help from Apollo," Mikolas replied.

Callie, Mel, and Tera came into the lobby from the main theater and wrapped Trinity in a tight group hug. Mikolas released her hand, basking in the glow of the muses. Together, these women were a force to be reckoned with. He was lucky to be in their orbit.

Callie stepped back to inspect Trinity. "You're okay?"

"Better off than my poor Guardian." She looked back at Mikolas, and the shine in her eyes had uninjured parts of him eager to get her alone. She faced her muse sisters again. "So tell me about Zack, or Zeus, whoever he was tonight."

Mel's face brightened, which for the Muse of Tragic Poetry was an unusual sight. "Oh, wait until you see Zack without his old-guy disguise. His skin has this radiance. He's *really* Zeus."

While they chatted, Rhea crossed to Mikolas and pulled him a couple of steps away from the others. "My son has a plan to convince his father that the human race is valuable."

Mikolas bit his cheek to keep from telling her how

insulting her words were. "How does he plan to do that?"

"A game." She rolled her eyes.

"A game?" So fucking typical of the gods. He wanted to scream, but it wouldn't change anything.

She nodded. "Your future depends on Zeus winning a game of Petteia."

Mikolas did his best to maintain a neutral expression. "Why are you telling me this?"

"Because now my fate also hangs in the balance. If Zeus loses, we will both be subjected to my husband's wrath."

Mikolas rubbed his forehead. "Iapetus almost killed three Guardians tonight. We'd never be able to defeat Kronos, especially with his ability to stop time."

"No, you misunderstand me." She shook her head slowly. "I don't expect my husband to abide by the agreement. Even if my son wins, Kronos will seek to destroy us."

Mikolas watched Trinity laughing with the other muses, and his heart clenched. They'd sacrificed so much to open this place, to inspire others, only to have the immortals ruin everything.

His gaze cut back to Rhea. "Do you have a plan?"

"Yes." She took Mikolas's hand, desperation in her eyes. "Inspire him."

Mikolas frowned. "What?"

She gestured to the theater. "My son will bring Kronos here, to the big opening. Make him see past his yearning for vengeance. Give him a new passion." She looked over at Trinity and the others. "I've spent lifetimes with generations of my granddaughters. I've seen the magic when they're together. Humanity is much more than their mortality. There is a beauty in them. My son has always seen it. Help Kronos see it, too."

"How?"

She met his eyes. "Help them make the opening perfect. Help them inspire the world in order to save it."

CHAPTER 17

Trinity glanced over at Mikolas as she drove them back to his place. She'd made a quick pit stop at her house to grab a change of clothes. Mason and Clio weren't home yet. By the time they had finished at Crystal Peak and made it to the theater, Mikolas was in desperate need of a shower and rest, so they had ducked out. But Mikolas had barely said a word since they had left *Les Neuf Soeurs*. Maybe it was just the exhaustion and the trauma his body had been through. The whole day had been draining on all of them, especially him.

She clicked the button to open the garage door and drove inside, closing it behind them. He didn't move. She unfastened her seat belt and turned his way. "Are you all right?"

"Yes. No." He looked over at her. "Rhea told me something tonight and I'm trying to figure out what to do with the information."

Trinity raised a brow. "I know you probably have a concussion or something, but I told you I love you and I meant it. Whatever she said, it's not going to change anything."

He shook his head and met her eyes. "She put me in a horrible position. You have worked so hard for the *Les Neuf Soeurs* opening. I don't want to ruin that, but I also don't want secrets between us."

"Okay, now you're scaring me. What's going on?"

"There's no way to defeat Kronos physically." He sighed. "But Zeus believes he can beat him in a game and save humanity."

"Seriously?" Trinity's jaw dropped. "Our future depends on Zeus rolling a twelve?"

"It's not that kind of game, but essentially, yes. And Rhea doesn't believe her husband will abide by the rules of their deal anyway, even if Zeus wins."

He rested his head on the seat and stared up at the roof of the car. "After he wins, Zeus is planning on bringing Kronos to the opening on Friday. Rhea thinks that when the muses are all together in the theater, you'll be able to inspire Kronos to have mercy, to show him the wonder and value of humanity."

Her heart palpitated. She coughed, trying to force it back into a normal rhythm. "No pressure or anything."

He frowned. "That's why I thought I should keep the information to myself."

"No." Trinity shook her head. "I'm glad you told me, but…wow."

"It's an unfair burden to be placed on your shoulders when changing the vengeful heart of the Father of the Gods may not even be possible."

She rested her hand on his thigh, her gaze locked

on his. "I'm still glad you told me."

"Should we tell the others?"

There was the million-dollar question. Her muse sisters were still riding high from their victory over Iapetus and finding out Zeus had finally gotten involved. They could focus on the opening without constantly looking over their shoulders for the next threat. How could she take that from them?

And even if they knew the stakes, Mikolas was right. It might be impossible to bring Kronos over to Team Human anyway.

Her decision was made. "No. There's nothing they can do differently anyway. If these are our last moments on Earth, I want my sisters to enjoy them to the fullest. No regrets and no pressure."

He leaned in and kissed her with a tenderness that melted her heart. "Words aren't big enough, but they're all that I have. *S'agapó.* I love you with all that I am."

She rested her forehead on his. "I love you, too. And if everything ends on Friday at the opening, I don't want to have any regrets, either."

His eyes sparkled in the dim dome light of the car. "I might need help reaching my back in the shower."

"Maybe I better shower with you." She bit her lower lip. "For safety's sake."

He kissed her again, his tongue parting her lips as his fingers tangled in her hair. She moaned into his mouth, aching to be even closer.

He broke the kiss, breathless as he met her eyes. "I want you naked in my arms."

She smiled. "I don't think your body is up for sex."

He glanced at the bulge in his pants and back to her. "I think parts of my body are."

She laughed, and it felt so damned good, she almost cried. "Let's get inside. I'll help you shower, and then we can see how you're feeling."

He opened his door. "I love hearing you laugh."

She grinned as she rounded the car to help him out. "You inspire me."

MIKOLAS STEPPED UNDER the hot water of the oversized marble shower. The multidirectional showerheads massaged his aching body as he wet his hair and pushed it back from his eyes. The dried blood from his shoulder wound vanished down the drain, washing away the evidence of how close he'd come to dying tonight.

Trinity slipped into the shower with him and chuckled, her smile lighting up her beautiful face. "Okay, this is an *amazing* shower. You could fit five people in here."

He clasped his hands on either side of her hips and brought her in closer to him. "You're the only person I want to share my shower with."

She smiled, running her hands up his wet chest.

"Lucky me." Her gaze darted to his shoulder, and her eyes widened. "Rhea's mark is gone."

He nodded. "Apparently I should have died as Achilles did when he was shot in the heel. Apollo changed my fate, but his healing must've lifted the blessing, too."

She pressed a kiss over his heart. "I thought I lost you tonight." She looked up at him from under her dark lashes, her skin shiny, wet, and oh so tempting. "I used to think that saying 'You don't know what you've got until it's gone' was a cliché. But I was wrong. It's *super* true."

He kissed her forehead. "When Apollo's power shot through me, I could hear your song. I've never experienced such intense pain, but as much as my body ached to surrender, your voice gave me the strength to fight." He pulled back enough to see her face. "I'm weak and battered, but I'm still not ready to give up. I want more time with you. I want a future."

"I want that, too." She reached up to bring him down for a kiss, but his ribs pinched. He straightened, laughing and cursing all at once. "Dammit. Rhea couldn't give me one more dose of healing energy?"

Trinity put some shower gel on a loofa and worked it into a foam. "We'll just have to be careful, and you'll have to let me do the work."

Her sexy smile had his erection reminding him once more that not *all* parts of his body were injured. She turned him around, running the loofa up his back in tender, gentle circles.

She sucked in a breath. "Probably for the best that you can't see your back. It's as if you got struck by lightning or something. You've got a modern masterpiece in the veins back here." She worked lower, caressing his ass. "Thankfully your perfect backside seems unscathed."

He tensed his glutes, and she rewarded him with her musical laughter. His heart swelled. But bitterness threatened to swallow his joy. It was fucking unfair to finally win her trust, her love, only to have an immortal destroy the world.

She pressed her lips to his back, and his anger dissipated, replaced by a surge of gratitude. Even if he only got to enjoy her for a few days, he was luckier than most. He turned around to face her again, running his wet hands up her waist. "I'm aching to kiss you, but bending seems to be an issue at the moment."

"Next time I'll bring a step stool."

He chuckled, careful not to jar his ribs. "You're such a gift, Trin."

He cupped her breasts, enjoying the weight of them in his hands as he toyed with her nipples until they hardened into tight nubs. She set the loofa aside and ran her soapy hands down his thighs. Her gaze remained locked on his as she bent her knees. Her full lips parted, and she slowly took him into her mouth, humming as her tongue teased his shaft.

His legs trembled, but he stayed upright. He buried

his hands in her wet hair. The warmth of her mouth was heaven. She slid her hands around him and gripped his ass, her lips gliding along his length faster. Gods, he wanted to lift her up and bury himself inside her. The pleasure and the torment of not being able to move only heightened the intensity.

He dropped his head back, closing his eyes, struggling to keep from surrendering. Not yet. His erection pulsed against her tongue. He pulled his hips back, sliding free from her lips. "I'm too close."

She smiled. "This may the only way we can do this tonight. Your ribs are too sore. Let me finish."

"My ribs are fine." Far from true, but his desire for her outweighed his body aches.

He washed her hair, her grateful moans keeping his erection throbbing and ready. Damn, he'd never wanted any woman so urgently in his life. They rinsed off and he wrapped a towel around his waist.

He took her hand, walking her over to the bed while attempting to calculate a position that wouldn't hurt his ribs. Tough to think straight when all his blood was rushing away from his brain, though. "I think if I sit on the edge of the bed I won't crush my ribs."

She raised a brow. "And me straddling your lap isn't going to hurt anything?"

He grinned and yanked her towel free. "We won't know unless we try."

Trinity waited for him to sit and then stood in front of him, stroking his erection. She ran her finger around the tip, drinking in the pleasure on his face. He froze, and she frowned. "Is this hurting you?"

"No." He shook his head. "I forgot a condom. They're in the bathroom."

"Screw it." She swallowed the lump in her throat. "If we live long enough to deal with the consequences, then we'll count ourselves lucky."

He brought his hand up to caress her cheek. "It wouldn't be a consequence, *agapi mou*. It would be a blessing."

Her heart melted along with all her worries for the world. Right now, *they* were the world. Everything else faded away. Against all odds, they survived, and dammit, she loved him.

She came forward and straddled his lap. His big hands gripped her ass, holding her up. She rested her forehead against his, sliding him slowly inside her. She moaned as he filled her.

He kissed her, whispering, "My heart, my life, are yours."

"'Til the end of time," she breathed as she fused her lips to his.

They both understood the end might be coming soon, but even if it didn't come for decades, it wouldn't be long enough. She'd never get enough of him. She worked her hips, sliding along his length, careful not to jar his chest. The effort had her muscles tight, sweat beading on her forehead.

And it felt so damned good. She'd had sex before, but this was…this was *making love*. This was celebrating being alive.

He nibbled his way down her neck, his hand sliding between them, rubbing gently at first until he found the spot that made her breath catch. "Right there," she gasped.

She ground her hips into him faster as he coaxed her closer to surrender. Her lips brushed his ear. "Look at me," she whispered.

He lifted his head, his gaze locked on hers. The intensity in his eyes, the emotions that played on his battered features, called to her. Her inner muscles clenched around him. "Come with me."

It was all the permission he needed. He erupted deep inside her, his body trembling, but their eyes never strayed. She'd never shared an intimate moment like this so honestly with anyone. It left her heart bare, but there was no trace of fear, no urge to cover her vulnerabilities. She didn't have to. From the core of her being, she knew he would protect her, just as she'd do the same for him.

"I love you, Trinity. Always." His voice was deep, throaty, and raw.

She kissed him, tangling her fingers in the back of

his hair. "I love you, too."

He deepened the kiss, his tongue parting her lips. His hands moved up her back, holding her tighter until he groaned and pulled back. "Dammit." He winced, shaking his head. "I think I need to lie down."

She helped him into the bed and crawled in beside him. "That was amazing. If you didn't have cracked ribs, you might have killed me."

He chuckled and opened his arms. "Come here."

She eyed his chiseled, black-and-blue chest. "You sure I won't hurt you if I snuggle in?"

He grinned. "It won't if you're gentle."

She waggled her eyebrows playfully. "Oh, I can be gentle."

He laughed and cringed. "Come here."

She lay in his arms with a goofy smile on her face that felt like it might never go away. She'd never dreamed she could feel this way.

He kissed her hair. "Will you move in with me?"

She lifted her head, staring down at him. "Seriously?"

"I know it's fast, but considering we may only have a few days left…"

Gods, he was right.

He ran his finger along her jaw. "I want to spend every second I have left with you."

She turned to kiss his fingertip. "Me too."

He raised a brow with a sexy grin that had part of her that should be exhausted perking up. "Is that a yes?"

"It's a hell yes." The last two words were breathy, teasing him. But she meant it.

He smiled and pulled her in for a slow kiss. "Let's laugh and love until the world ends."

"Deal." She settled against his chest, her eyes drifting closed.

He stroked her shoulder. "Does that mean you'll come with me to pick up my grandparents in the morning?"

Trinity lifted her head and grinned. "I can't wait to meet them."

He chuckled. "They're going to love you."

CHAPTER 18

Mikolas scanned the line of people coming down the escalator toward baggage claim. Trinity was beside him, holding his hand. She nudged him with her hip. "Tell me about them."

He smiled just thinking of his grandparents. "Nona loves to cook, and she's the Muse of Astronomy, so do *not* indulge her with stargazing unless you're prepared to be up all night." He chuckled, looking over at Trinity. "She's never been to America and her English is a little rough, but that won't stop her from trying to show you every constellation."

"She's going to love the lights on the ceiling of the theater lobby."

He nodded. "She's going to love *everything* about your theater."

"And your grandfather?"

"Papou filled my head with stories about the gods and goddesses from the time I was a little boy. It was his idea to send me undercover into the Order of the Titans to stop them from freeing Kronos. The gods have never been a myth to my grandfather; he's always been a believer. Ah!" Mikolas noticed them at the top of the escalator. "There they are."

He pointed toward an elderly man wearing a Hawaiian shirt with surfboards all over it, and his nona was right beside him in a bright-yellow top with a white straw hat. She spotted Mikolas and waved.

Mikolas squeezed Trinity's hand and led her over to meet them at the bottom of the escalator. He embraced them both and tried to pull away to introduce Trinity, but Nona wasn't going to let him get away yet.

She pinched his cheek. "Miko! You're too skinny." She noticed the cut on his eyebrow and frowned. "You're hurt."

He chuckled. His ribs, thankfully, didn't protest as much this morning. "You should see the other guy."

His grandfather shook his head. "I'm sorry the gods didn't give you my gift, Miko."

"I'm fine." He reached for Trinity, pulling her closer to him. "This is Trinity, my muse."

He stepped back as his grandparents suffocated her with hugs and peppered her with questions. She smiled at him and did her best to field every query. How could he possibly love her more?

But he did. With every second.

His grandmother insisted on visiting the theater first, so Mikolas loaded their luggage in the trunk as they got into his car. He and Trinity had agreed not to darken the excitement of the theater opening with revealing Rhea's dire warning, but seeing his grandparents made it impossible to ignore what would happen if Kronos destroyed everything. He'd never see his parents or his home in Greece ever again.

He rubbed the ache in his chest and pushed the dark thoughts to the back of his mind. Hopefully the others would be at the theater, working on last-minute preparations for the opening. Staying busy made it easier live in the present instead of worrying about the future.

As Mikolas parked in the newly paved theater lot, Zack was helping an elderly woman out of his car. Mikolas frowned and glanced at Trinity. "He's disguised again. And who is that with him?"

Trinity surprised him, turning around to his grandmother. "Mrs. Leandros?"

"Call me Nona," she said in her heavy Greek accent.

Trinity smiled. "Nona, our generation lost the Muse of Astronomy and the Muse of Hymns, but the woman over there is from your generation. Her name is Agnes Hanover. She's the Muse of Hymns."

His grandmother's eyes widened, and she reached for the door handle. In Greek, she rambled on about all nine muses and how she'd never found any of her sisters. Before Trinity could say another word, Nona was out of the Mercedes and heading for Mrs. Hanover.

Mikolas chuckled, shaking his head. "We didn't get to tell her the old man is really Zeus."

His grandfather coughed. "What?"

Mikolas nodded. "This is his disguise to blend into our world, but that's Zeus. He calls himself Zack Vrontios."

His grandfather smiled. *"Thunder,"* he said, translating Zack's last name aloud. "He still walks among the mortals. I should have known."

Mikolas opened his door. "We should have warned Nona."

"It is better this way, Miko." With a twinkle in his eye, his grandfather grinned.

Mikolas came around the car and took Trinity's hand. His brow furrowed for a moment, suddenly realizing something. "Hanover... That's Cooper's last name, isn't it?"

"Yep." She squeezed his hand. "She's his grandmother."

Mikolas raised a brow. "Are any of the other Guardians related to muses?"

"Clio told me Mason had an older cousin who was the Muse of Music." She lowered her voice. "Philyra drowned her when he was just a little boy. He was hunting her. That's what brought him to Crystal City in the first place."

"I wonder how long Zeus has been planning for this day. From birth, we've all been pawns on his chessboard." Mikolas stared at Zack in his purple hooligan hat. As if he could sense Mikolas, Zack turned and met his gaze, then tugged on the brim in greeting.

Trinity squeezed Mikolas's hand, pulling his attention back to her. "Don't waste your time being angry."

She was right. Time was precious. He lifted their joined hands to his lips and kissed her knuckles. "Thank you."

She winked. "We make a good team."

By the time they caught up with Nona and Mrs. Hanover, the two muses were hugging. A tear rolled down Nona's cheek as she stepped back.

Mrs. Hanover dabbed the corner of her eye. "We were on opposite sides of the world all this time."

Nona nodded and reached for Trinity's hand. "The theater was not in our generation's destiny, but we can still help them. They only have seven. We can make them complete."

Cooper's grandmother blinked. "Oh, do you need help with the opening?"

Trinity smiled. "Actually, we were hoping you might want to get involved."

The three women walked toward the theater hand in hand with Trinity in the middle, leaving Mikolas behind with his grandfather and Zeus. Papou eyed Zack warily, so Mikolas turned to Zack to introduce them. "Zack, this is my grandfather—"

"Alexander, Guardian to Sofia," Zack finished for him. He came forward and offered his hand.

Mikolas's grandfather stood slack-jawed, his English halted and broken. "You are…truly… They tell me you are, but I…can't…understand…You're—"

"Zeus." For a moment, Zack allowed his disguise to

fade. His skin glowed as if the sun radiated from inside his chest instead of up in the sky, his eyes sparking with power. "Thank you for protecting Sofia and for sending Mikolas to the other side of the world. Without you, we would have no hope of defending this world from my father's wrath."

His grandfather nodded and took Zeus's hand as he morphed back into Zack. "Ah, you are old again."

Zack laughed and pulled Mikolas's grandfather in for a tight hug. He released him and stepped back. "It's easier to blend in. And I can't seem like a threat." The immortal sobered, looking at both of them. "Eons ago, the Guiders of Destiny predicted my father's escape from Tartarus, and they foresaw the danger to my daughters. I brought them into the world every generation, knowing it might take more than one generation to complete this mission. Seeing it all come to fruition is…satisfying."

"Satisfying?" Mikolas stared at the King of Olympians, shaking his head and struggling to rein in his frustration. He put his arm around his grandfather's shoulders, his gaze locked on Zack. "I realize that to you we're just playthings in some cosmic game, but I *love* that woman, who embodies the spirit of one of your daughters. I would die for Trinity. For us, this isn't a game."

Zack raised a brow, his tone stern. "I have mourned every death."

"Maybe so, but I'm telling you this 'plan' you've

been working on for centuries is being played out by people of flesh and blood. We won't live forever like you, so the time we have is precious, the people are priceless. Two of Trinity's friends are dead. So maybe hold off on being satisfied until all of your daughters are safe."

Papou nudged him. "Miko... You are speaking to Zeus."

"I know who he is, Papou. He marked me to be Trinity's Guardian and laid out my destiny before I was born, but I want it to be crystal clear that I'm not fighting for the gods, or for humanity, or for Zeus." He pointed to Trinity and his grandmother as they stood in front of the painting of Urania on the outside of the building. "I'll fight because I love those two women over there, and love is the *only* thing worth fighting for."

Before he said something that Zeus might make him live to regret, he broke free of his grandfather and started toward Trinity.

ZEUS WATCHED MIKOLAS walk away, a smile tugging at his lips. Pulling the golden thread through time, marking honorable men to be Guardians, had been a heavy responsibility, but Mikolas Leandros was proof that Zeus had chosen wisely. The mortal stood before him, knowing Zeus could strike him down at any time, and he still spoke his truth, protected his muse.

Love was a complicated emotion for gods with limitless time, but humans cherished it for the gift it was meant to be. They experienced the pain of its loss in a way that immortals struggled to understand.

He shifted his gaze to Alexander. The Guardian was older now, his hair thinning and gray. Deep lines marred his tan skin around his eyes and forehead. In spite of the years, Alexander lifted his chin and squared his shoulders with a keen glint in his eye.

"I raised my grandson on stories of the gods and goddesses. I taught Miko to respect the role of fate and destiny, but he is right in this." Alexander crossed his arms over his chest. "Love gives our lives meaning. Our stories may never be immortalized in the stars like yours, but Sofia's life is written in my heart and it will be until it stops beating. So whatever game you're playing with your father, stop deciding who wins and loses, and learn something from my grandson. Try loving each other instead."

Alexander walked away next, trailing after Mikolas and leaving Zeus behind with much to think about.

TRINITY GRINNED AS she led Mikolas's grandmother into the lobby. Sofia Leandros definitely carried the spark of Urania in her soul. She exuded light in her smile, her laughter, even in her stubborn attitude. Now

Trinity knew where Mikolas got it from.

Sofia stared at the multitude of tiny sparkling lights spiraling around pages of music and hymns to fill the expanse of the high ceiling. Pure joy warmed her features as she grinned and clasped her hands together. "Beautiful. As if the light of inspiration and music floats up to the stars." She pulled her gaze back to Trinity's face. "This theater is perfect. Just like the one in my dreams."

Trinity beamed with a pride she hadn't expected to feel from Nona's approval. "You haven't even seen all of it yet." She took Nona's arm, and Agnes followed on her other side. Although she didn't know the older women well, that connection, the shared experience of discovering the yearning to inspire, bonded her to them. They were muses, regardless of generation.

Callie met them on the stage, and Trinity introduced Mikolas's grandmother. Callie welcomed them and glanced at Trinity. "Have you asked them yet?"

Trinity shook her head. "You're our fearless leader. I just brought them to you."

Callie rolled her eyes but still managed to smile warmly. "Fine." She looked at Sofia and Agnes. "We were hoping you two might join us onstage at the opening, so all nine muses would be represented."

Sofia grinned, nodding. "This is why I come from Greece, to help you…to shine light. Urania."

Trinity looked over at Agnes and held her breath. Cooper's grandmother was her generation's Polyhymnia, but she was also shy. Putting her onstage in front of a packed house might be too far outside her comfort zone. Being a muse hadn't been a gift during Agnes's lifetime. Her Guardian had never found her, and her husband had never understood the muse inside her. She was a widow now, but she'd buried that part of herself for so long that Trinity wasn't sure she could truly let Polyhymnia out anymore.

Sofia reached for Agnes's hand and gave it a squeeze. "Sister, let's help them inspire the world."

"Sister…" A slow smile curved over Agnes's lips as the stage lights shone in her watery eyes. "I've waited a lifetime for this."

The older women embraced again, and Trinity slid her arm around Callie's waist with a knowing look. "Remember how amazing it felt when we finally found each other?"

Callie nodded. "Instant family."

Once all the muses arrived and were introduced, Callie led the rehearsal. They ran through entrances, music, dances, sing-alongs, and readings. While they worked, Mikolas sat in the back row of the orchestra seats, his dark eyes following Trinity's every move. One by one, the others joined him. Hunter, Cooper, Nate, Mason, Gavin, Mikolas's grandfather, and even Reed, filled the row beside Mikolas.

Family. Maybe not by blood, but definitely by destiny.

"Great job today everyone!" Callie said from centerstage. "We've got a few more days to shake out the kinks, but it's going to be great. See you all back here tomorrow."

Trinity sat at the piano working through some chords while the others said their good-byes and left. She closed her eyes, surrendering to the melody. As her fingers settled on the final chord, she pressed the sustain pedal, sending the music echoing into the ether.

Two heavy hands rested on her shoulders. She tipped her head back and smiled up at Mikolas. "Are we finally alone?"

He bent down, pressing a kiss to her forehead. "My grandparents are waiting in the car."

"They're amazing."

He nodded, taking her hand and helping her up from the piano bench. "They love you already."

She sobered. "Today was… I don't have words. Being with those women, seeing you out there with all the guys who have worked so hard to help us make this happen…" She stared at the ceiling. "If this is the end…" She met his eyes with a smile. "What a way to go, right?"

He wrapped her in a warm embrace she wished she could stay in forever. He kissed her hair and then kept his deep voice low, for her ears only, as he said, "I don't believe our story is ending. I can't."

She pulled back enough to see his entire face. "Did Zack tell you something I should know?"

"No." He pointed to the back row of seats. "But I sat out there for hours today, and it seemed like seconds. All nine muse sisters together on that stage is a magic I never realized existed. You made me believe anything is possible. I think all of us felt it. This place… One of them called a beacon." He shook his head and met her eyes. "It's magic here, Trin. Friday is going to be spectacular. If anything could save humanity in the eyes of the God of Time, it's the nine Muses."

She buried her face in his chest, clinging to him as a tear slid down her cheek. "You have no idea how much I want you to be right."

"Let's get my grandparents settled at the hotel so I can take you home." A sexy smile curved his lips, and heat blossomed low in her belly.

"Deal."

CHAPTER 19

Friday came much too soon. Zack waited under a shady tree at the park, his ivory game board already set up. Americans probably assumed it was checkers with the white and black discs in rows on either side of the black and white squares of the board, but Petteia was thousands of years older.

He stared at the empty chair across the table. He'd replayed this day in his head countless times. If he had it to do all over again, would he have attacked his father when his mother asked him to? Was destiny unavoidable?

He'd learned so much from his own daughters in the eons since. For generations, he'd passed in and out of their lives. Instead of jealousy and petty infighting, these muses taught him about love and respect, things he'd never found on the heights of Olympus. In that time, he'd come to realize something: he wasn't the hero of the story. Not really. He'd had the might, and the numbers, but was it heroic to punish his father as his mother had pressured him to do? More importantly, did it even matter anymore? Fighting the same battle for control seemed…pointless.

Alexander Leandros's parting words had haunted Zack for days. *Could* they learn to love each other instead of deeming one a victor and the other a loser? Truth be told, he wasn't sure his vengeful father was capable of love. Maybe it was too late for redemption for two forgotten gods in this world of mankind.

Kronos approached the table. Like Zeus, his father wore his mortal disguise. Kevin Elys was tall and slender, and although his hair was silver and wrinkles lined his eyes, the immortal power of the God of Time was present.

He took off his coat and laid it over the back of the chair before taking a seat. "You're older than I remember, boy."

"I could say the same to you," he countered. "I wasn't certain you would come."

"Where else would I be? The chance to defeat you is the only reason I came back to this world." He glanced at the board in front of him. "I must say I expected our rematch to be on a more *epic* scale."

"This is the world of man now. I don't seek to make a spectacle with lightning bolts anymore."

His father raised a brow. "I find that hard to believe."

Zack pulled in a slow breath. "I've changed over the millennia that have passed. Why punish mortals for our shortcomings?"

His father made his first move, pushing a black disc forward on the board. "If this is humanity's world, then

I really am Kevin Elys."

"Elys." Zeus slid his white disc next to Kevin's. "For the Elysian fields?"

Kevin's eyes sparked, flashing his immortal power for a moment. "You're the first person to pick up on that."

"Most humans don't remember the story of the Elysian fields, Father."

"Enough." Kevin lifted his hand. "I'm sick of hearing you call me father. You lost that right the day you put that poison in my cup." He moved a second piece next to Zack's, trapping it between the black pieces. He removed it from the board with a smirk. "This will be *my* world very soon."

Zack crossed his arms and leaned back in his chair. "I only poisoned your cup in order to free my siblings. You held them in your stomach for years over a prophecy that you would be overthrown by one of your children."

"A *true* prophecy, as we came to see." He pointed to the board. "Make your move."

"You brought it to fruition with your paranoia." Zack rested his hands on either side of the table. "It didn't have to be that way."

"Says you." He shook his head. "Make your move. I have a brother to avenge."

Zack stared across the table at his father, and an idea crystalized in his mind. "You loved Iapetus," he said, thinking out loud.

Kevin raised his gaze to Zack's face. "He was my brother."

"But you experienced pain when we felt him vanish from this plane. You miss him. That's love." Zack gestured to a couple wandering about the park, oblivious to the fact that their fate was being decided by two old men at a gaming table. "Mortals understand this secret we struggle to comprehend. They cherish those they love because unlike us, time is finite for them."

"It doesn't matter. They killed my brother. They'll pay with their lives." He broke eye contact, focusing on the board instead. "Go."

"When my mother finally brought me into your presence for the first time, I wanted your acceptance, your praise, so badly." Zack didn't take his turn. Rather, he waited for his father to look at him. "When you made me your cupbearer instead of your son, that rejection festered in me. I could have loved you. Instead, hate grew."

Kevin leaned back in his chair. "What is this game you're playing?"

"It's not a game." Zack chuckled flatly, allowing a grim smile to curve his lips. "Why must we always have a winner and a loser? What if we learned to love each other instead?"

Kevin didn't offer a quick comeback. His stare was heavy, shielded, leaving Zack to wonder what was going through his father's head. But in the silence, Zack realized his words hadn't been a manipulation or a game. They'd been honest.

Even after the passage of thousands of years, he still ached for his father's approval.

"Your mother and I wanted children. We envisioned we would fill this world with incredible beings, parts of us." Stroking his chin, Kevin met Zack's eyes. "That prophecy poisoned me, my marriage, my family. From the moment I heard it, the only thing that mattered was keeping it from happening. Rhea was so excited when she found out she was expecting our child, but I came to see every pregnancy as a betrayal."

Zack crossed his arms. "Don't succumb to it again. This is a new chance for a new world."

"Even if I wanted that, my path is set." A muscle ticked in his cheek. "I will see humanity punished for taking my brother's life, and I will see you and your mother disgraced and degraded for your treachery." He nudged the board. "Make your move, boy."

"I have." Zack slid all his pieces off the board. This wasn't a game. Not anymore. "I'm far from perfect, just like you, but I'm willing to forget the past and look to a new future with my father."

Kevin's laughter was cold as he shook his head. "Then you're a fool."

"Perhaps. But before you mete out your punishment, come with me to *Les Neuf Soeurs* for its opening. Let your granddaughters show you the beauty of humanity. Their lives are short, but they have worth."

"So I have won." Kevin wiped his markers off the

board. "And when I go to the theater with you, you and your mother will face me."

"We never finished the game. No winner and no loser." He tugged on the brim of his purple hat. "And we will embrace you at the theater, if you allow it."

His father laughed again, but there was no joy in his eyes. "Your mother will never embrace me."

"Not as long as you seek to hurt her, but maybe if you remembered how to love her she would. The prophecy is long dead. Forgotten as a myth. Let's leave it there."

Kevin stood, his movements stiff. "I'm finished talking."

Zack nodded, picked up the board, and stopped beside his father. "Then let's move forward."

"I've agreed to nothing."

"We walk away together without a winner or loser." Zack moved down the path with his father at his side and his immortal heart pounding in his ears. "That's enough for me."

CHAPTER 20

Trinity stood centerstage, alone in the heat of the spotlight. She was frozen in time but not by Kronos. She glanced toward the wings. Mikolas smiled at her, his strength and love bathing her as much as the lights were.

She took a bow and sat on the piano bench. The audience applauded offered their energy to the moment as she placed her hands on the keys. The first chord rang out, echoing through the space like a bolt of lightning. Inspiration poured from her fingers, the piano strings converting it into a living thing, a force of nature, something magical.

She leaned into the mic, adding her voice to the song. This one she'd written for her sisters, for their struggles and their commitment, their devotion to inspiring humanity to love instead of hate, to help others instead of judge them, to create and be brave enough to share it with the world.

All her worries vanished into the melody. Anything was possible. Humanity was worth the fight. Life was messy, full of pain and pleasure…. And love… Gods, love was worth every heartbreak, every loss. She knew that now.

As Trinity played, her sisters began to join her onstage, singing the chorus along with her. Clio and Lia entered from stage left, and Mel and Callie from stage right. Then Tera came dancing up the center aisle of the theater, and right behind her, Sofia and Agnes walked down the aisle hand in hand.

The spotlight followed them toward the stage, casting long shadows across the audience. The muses began to clap to beat of the music, and finally Erica entered with a cordless microphone, completing the sisterhood, all nine muses together inspiring mankind again after millennia apart.

She stood in the crook of the piano and faced the full house. "Please join us. Move, dance, clap, sing—the world needs our magic. You all have a story to tell, a history to write however you choose. Your ideas will move us all into the future, a *better* future. We can make that happen. The world is what we make it, and it's worth fighting for."

Trinity and Mikolas hadn't shared the consequences of tonight's opening with anyone. Erica had no idea of the literal truth in her opening welcome. But Trinity wondered if immortals had witnessed Erica's speech.

With the spotlight on her, Trinity couldn't see the audience, couldn't see if Zeus and Kronos were in attendance, and suddenly, she realized she didn't give a shit.

Gods be damned.

They weren't going to ruin this moment or this alchemy of inspiration they were manifesting tonight. This was humanity's moment.

Trinity's vision wavered, blurred by tears as Erica turned around to face her. She came over and nudged her over on the piano bench, keeping the mic away from her mouth. "It's been too long since music and lyrics were together."

Trinity laid her head on her best friend's shoulder. "You always make me better."

"Right back atcha, Sister."

Trinity smiled as a tear slipped down her cheek. Erica brought the mic back up, placing it right between them as she took over the high notes on the keyboard with her right hand, while Trinity carried the chords. They harmonized their voices into the mic, sending the song into the air. Then an amazing thing happened: the back doors of the theater opened, and women of all ages, races, and backgrounds walked down the aisles toward the stage. The spotlight moved away from Trinity to the women entering the theater.

Trinity's chest clenched. They were muses. All of them. She had no idea how she knew, but she had. Instantly.

They united their voices, the song taking on its own life, unable to be contained by the walls of the theater. Erica gestured for them to come onstage. Trinity kept playing, but movement in the far-left corner of the audience caught her eye—Zeus and Kronos. And on the other side…Rhea.

Trinity didn't understand what was happening. Was this it? Was the world about to end?

She stopped playing, but the singing went on. Trinity jogged offstage into the wings and embraced Mikolas. "They're out there." He tensed, starting to turn, but she didn't let him go. "Wait. I want you with me. Please."

He stared into her eyes and finally nodded. "Okay."

She took his hand, bringing him out to the piano. The singing faded as she reached for the mic. "Thanks for being here tonight. It's been so much more than we ever expected, but there are some unsung heroes among us, and without them, this theater wouldn't be standing." She peered around the wings and out into the house for the Guardians. "Come on, you guys. Get up here."

Nate came onstage with Maggie and Noah in tow. Reed joined him with baby Hope in his arms. Cooper came out from the wings, and Mason followed, his tool belt still fastened around his waist. Hunter and Gavin came up from the audience with Mikolas's grandfather. The men joined their muses, and a wave of emotion washed through Trinity's heart.

She smiled up at Mikolas before she addressed the crowd again. "These guys believed in us even when everything seemed to be falling apart. Can we show them a little love?"

The roars from the crowd filled the space, and

through the noise and applause, an older gentleman gradually made his way to the stage. He had on khaki slacks, and a plaid shirt with a v-neck sweater. As he got closer, a smile warmed his face. He stopped in front of Agnes.

Trinity nudged Erica, and as if her best friend read her mind, she took the cordless mic over to him. "Do we know you?"

He took it, eyeing the black cylinder suspiciously before looking back up at Agnes. "Are you Agnes Hanover?"

Color flushed her pale skin as she nodded.

He lifted his other hand to his forehead, wiping away what could only be nervous sweat, and Trinity noticed the bright-red crescent-shaped mark on the back of his hand. Agnes's Guardian. It had to be. She bit her lip to keep quiet.

The older guy finally held the mic up again. "I'm Everett Seagle. I know this sounds crazy, but…I wasn't sure why I came here today until I saw you." He glanced over to the left corner of the theater and back to her. "Your friend Zack told me your name. I…I've never done anything like this before." His voice softened, as if the rest of the packed auditorium had vanished. "I've been searching for you my whole life. I never gave up."

The audience cheered as Hunter jogged down the stairs to help Everett come up on the stage. Trinity went to peer at the immortals at the back of the theater, but they were gone.

Whether it was a good sign or not, she had no idea. But she had hope. And tonight, that was enough.

EPILOGUE

Six months later – Nea Kardylia, Greece

TRINITY WALKED DOWN the dock, her flip-flops popping against the weathered wood planks. Their vacation was over. Tomorrow they'd be flying back to Crystal City, and then she could focus on songwriting again. She hadn't written anything new since the night Mikolas had almost died battling the Piercer.

Six months.

Gods, she'd never gone so long without a new melody in her heart. She tried not to panic. Maybe she just needed Erica to come up with some lyrics and it would flow again.

Mikolas had been quietly supportive, trying to give her time to write, buying her fancy notebooks and sheet music paper for her notations, but so far…nothing.

Thinking about it, and worrying, definitely wasn't helping her writer's block.

As they neared the end of the dock, she wrapped one arm around the bottom of her pregnant belly and the other slid around Mikolas's waist. "You were so lucky to grow up here, right on the banks of the Struma River. It's gorgeous."

"When I was younger, all I could think about was moving to a big city." He grinned, helping her into the rowboat.

Once she was seated, he got in and reached for the oars. "Are you ready to go home?"

"I guess so. I miss my sisters, but I have a hard time telling if it's me or if Euterpe is just excited to be back in Greece. It does feel like home here." She drank in the view of Mikolas's muscular shoulders and arms as he pulled the oars though the water and thought about what was waiting back in California for them.

The theater was still open, and no one had seen the immortals again since that first night. Rhea, Zack, and the Guiders of Destiny were all missing from Blessed Mary Village, and the mansion Kevin Elys had rented was empty and on the market. Mikolas had taken over Belkin Oil and closed their off-shore drilling division.

And she still hadn't written a single song. *Ugh!*

But she was grateful for each new day. Not only did the God of Time not wipe out humanity but she was going to have a baby soon with the man she loved more than she ever realized she could love anyone.

She leaned back, closing her eyes and soaking up the Mediterranean sun. The rhythmic squeak of the oars, the current of the water—it all blended into a symphony of sound. When the boat stopped at their dock, she shielded her eyes and peered up. A familiar face smiled down at her.

He tugged on the brim of his purple hat. "You're glowing."

Her jaw dropped as she looked over at Mikolas. "Did you know Zeus was here?"

Mikolas smiled. "He asked me not to say anything, and since he saved the world, I thought I would indulge him."

Zack shook his head. "I didn't save the world. Love did."

Mikolas helped her out of the boat. Once she was on the dock, she hugged the Olympian and stepped back. "We're naming the baby Zeus, even if it's a girl."

"She's going to change the world," he said with a wink.

Trinity looked up at Mikolas and back to Zack. "Okay, so maybe I was kidding about naming her Zeus...Maybe Zoe." She grinned. "So where have you been? What happened the night of the theater opening?"

"Alexander gave me the key to ending the battle. My father and I spent eons fighting for dominance when all we really wanted was acceptance and respect. I planted the seed, but you, your sisters, and your Guardians inspired him and my mother to try again." He took Trinity's hand. "I came to say thank you."

She started to reply when his disguise faded. His true form, a being of light and energy, was blinding.

"Keep singing your songs, Trinity."

And then he was gone.

Mikolas took her hand, shaking his head. "He's still a show-off."

Trinity dropped her head back and laughed. Mikolas swept her up into his arms and started carrying her up the dock away from the river. She hooked her arms around his neck. "You're going to get a hernia lugging my pregnant butt all the way back to your parent's house."

"You're not that heavy." He smiled down at her. "I love you. *Both of you.*"

She rested her head against his chest, staring at her belly bulge as his heartbeat became the tempo for the only Greek tune she knew, his grandparent's song. She sang the words, and she would keep singing. When she left this world, her songs would live on in her children—*their* children.

She looked up at Mikolas and smiled. "Someday you'll have to tell me what the words mean."

He set her down on her feet when they reached the door and lifted her hand to his lips. "You are my sun, my moon, and stars. The gods gave you to me to cherish until the stars call us home."

"That's beautiful."

"It's not what the song means."

She raised a brow. "Then what is it?"

"It's my promise to you. I know everything happened quickly, and according to my grandfather, we're doing this backward, having a baby before we get married and all, but I want you to know how much you mean to me." He rested his hand on her belly. "I love you."

She tipped her chin up and kissed his lips. "We're lucky girls."

He chuckled. "I will do my best to make sure you always feel that way."

He opened the door, and they stepped inside to find his grandparents had dozed off in front of the television, still holding hands. Her heart melted.

And suddenly a new melody whispered through her soul. Her eyes brimmed with grateful tears. The music was back. Inspiration had struck.

Mikolas frowned at the tears welling in her eyes, but she rose up on her toes, kissing him before he could ask what was wrong.

The answer was nothing. Everything was just right.

The song was simple, like his grandparents falling asleep holding hands. Life was messy and uncertain, but love made every second worthwhile.

She tasted his lips once more before pulling back and smiling up at him. "I think I need a pen."

Acknowledgments

Thank you for reading Song of the Soul and if you enjoyed the story I hope you'll post a review online. Even short reviews help readers find books.

Song of the Soul was such a joy to write. Wrapping up a series is always emotional for me, like telling my best friends goodbye, but this one left me feeling uplifted and so grateful that I got to write these books. The Muses, and their sisterhood, have been a thrill from the first book to the last, and I'm so grateful to all of you for coming along on the adventure with me!

First off, I need to thank my editor, Danielle Poiesz from Double Vision Editorial for helping me with this entire series. You always make me better and help me pull out depth from every character. This was our first complete series together and I already can't wait to start the next one.

I also want to give a shout out to my terrific cover artist, Fiona Jayde, for all her work on this series and making all the Guardians look so good. Thanks for making all the tweaks and never getting sick of my questions.

And huge thanks to my intrepid beta readers for this book, Denise Vance Fluhr and Heather Cox, who read this book so fast for me. You guys are the best!

Big thanks to my Night Angel readers on Facebook. You all cheered me on through this book and the entire series. Your encouragement keeps me sane!

This entire series was inspired by a short story I wrote called, Unemployed Muses Anonymous, during my 52 stories in 52 weeks challenge that Ray Bradbury had suggested. So far, his writing tip has yielded two different series, totaling fifteen novels, and I'll be forever grateful to him for his sage advice. To all the writers out there, never give up and give yourself the freedom to write short. You never know what might be inspired.

Last but never least, big thanks to my husband, Ken, for his never-ending patience while I brainstorm out loud about fictional characters. Your love and support make these books possible. I love you!

Other Novels by Lisa Kessler

The Muse Chronicles
LURE OF OBSESSION
LEGEND OF LOVE
BREATH OF PASSION
LIGHT OF THE SPIRIT
DEVOTED TO DESTINY
DANCE OF THE HEART
SONG OF THE SOUL

The Night Series
NIGHT WALKER
NIGHT THIEF
NIGHT DEMON
NIGHT ANGEL
NIGHT CHILD

The Moon Series
MOONLIGHT
HUNTER'S MOON
BLOOD MOON
HARVEST MOON
ICE MOON
BLUE MOON
WOLF MOON
NEW MOON

The Sedona Pack
SEDONA SIN
SEDONA SEDUCTION

The Sentinels of Savannah
MAGNOLIA MYSTIC
PIRATE'S PASSION

Summerland Stories
ACROSS THE VEIL
FORBIDDEN HEARTS

Stand Alone Works
BEG ME TO SLAY
FORGOTTEN TREASURES

Stay up-to-date on new releases and giveaways by subscribing to Lisa's newsletter here:
https://goo.gl/56lDla

Lisa Kessler is a Best Selling author of dark paranormal fiction. She's a two-time San Diego Book Award winner for Best Published Fantasy-Sci-fi-Horror and Best Published Romance. Her books have also won the PRISM award, the Award of Excellence, the National Excellence in Romantic Fiction Award, the Award of Merit from the Holt Medallion, and an International Digital Award for Best Paranormal.

Her short stories have been published in print anthologies and magazines, and her vampire story, Immortal Beloved, was a finalist for a Bram Stoker award.

When she's not writing, Lisa is a professional vocalist, and has performed with San Diego Opera as well as other musical theater companies in San Diego.

You can learn more at Lisa-Kessler.com

Made in the USA
Columbia, SC
04 September 2022